"We have challenges in front of us. I'd like to focus on them without…complications."

That part wasn't the whole truth, but it was certainly true enough.

It didn't matter. No more kissing. That was the rule and she was sticking to it.

"Caitlyn. You focus on your challenges your way, and I'll focus on my challenges my way."

"What's that supposed to mean?" she whispered, afraid she wasn't going to like the answer.

Antonio looked at her. "It means I'm going to kiss you again. You'd best think of another argument if you don't want me to."

Triplets
Under the Tree

KAT CANTRELL

First published in Great Britain 2016
by Mills & Boon, an imprint of Harlequin (UK) Limited,
Large Print edition 2016
Eton House, 18-24 Paradise Road,
Richmond, Surrey, TW9 1SR

© 2015 Kat Cantrell

ISBN: 978-0-263-06624-1

Printed and bound in Great Britain
by CPI Antony Rowe, Chippenham, Wiltshire

Kat Cantrell read her first Harlequin novel in third grade and has been scribbling in notebooks since she learned to spell. What else would she write but romance? She majored in literature, officially with the intent to teach, but somehow ended up buried in middle management in corporate America, until she became a stay-at-home mom and full-time writer.

Kat, her husband and their two boys live in north Texas. When she's not writing about characters on the journey to happily-ever-after, she can be found at a soccer game, watching the TV show *Friends* or listening to '80s music.

Kat was the 2011 Harlequin So You Think You Can Write contest winner and a 2012 RWA Golden Heart Award finalist for best unpublished series contemporary manuscript.

To Diane Spigonardo.
Thanks for the inspiration.

Prologue

Near Punggur Besar, Batam Island, Indonesia

Automatically, Falco swung his arm in an arc to block the punch. He hadn't seen it coming. But a sense he couldn't explain told him to expect his opponent's attack.

Counterpunch. His opponent's head snapped backward. *No mercy.* Flesh smacked flesh again and again, rhythmically.

The moves came to him fluidly, without thought. He'd been learning from Wilipo for only a few months, but Falco's muscles already sang with expertise, adopting the techniques easily.

His opponent, Ravi, attacked yet again. Falco

ducked and spun to avoid the hit. His right leg ached with the effort, but he ignored it. It always ached where the bone had broken.

From his spot on the sidelines of the dirt-floored ring, Wilipo grunted. The sound meant more footwork, less jabbing.

Wilipo spoke no English and Falco had learned but a handful of words in Bahasa since becoming a student of the sole martial arts master in southern Batam Island. Their communication during training sessions consisted of nods and gestures. A blessing, considering Falco had little to say.

The stench of old fish rent the air, more pungent today with the heat. Gazes locked, Falco and Ravi circled each other. The younger man from a neighboring village had become Falco's sparring partner a week ago after he'd run out of opponents in his own village. The locals whispered about him and he didn't need to speak Bahasa to understand they feared him.

He wanted to tell them not to be afraid. But he knew he was more than a strange Westerner in an Asian village full of simple people. More than a man with dangerous fists.

Nearly four seasons ago, a fisherman had found

Falco floating in the water, unconscious, with horrific injuries. At least that was what he'd pieced together from the doctor's halting, limited English.

He should have died before he'd washed ashore in Indonesia and he certainly should have died at some point during the six-month coma his body had required to heal.

But he'd lived.

And when he finally awoke, it was to a nightmare of physical rehabilitation and confusion. His memories were fleeting. Insubstantial. Incomplete. He was the man with no past, no home, no idea who he was other than angry and lost.

The only clue to his identity lay inked across his left pectoral muscle—a fierce, bold falcon tattoo with a scarlet banner clutched in his talons, emblazoned with the word *Falco*. That was what his saviors called him since he didn't remember his name, though it chafed to be addressed as such.

Why? It must be a part of his identity. But when he pushed his memory, it only resulted in his fists primed to punch something and a blinding headache. Every waking moment—and even some of those dedicated to sleep—he heard an urgent soul-deep cry to discover why he'd been snatched from the teeth of a cruel death. Surely he'd lived for a reason. Surely he'd remember something critical to set him on the path toward who he was. Every day thus far had ended in disappointment.

Only fighting allowed him moments of peace and clarity as he disciplined his mind to focus on something other than the struggle to remember.

Ravi and Wilipo spoke in rapid Bahasa, leaving the Westerner out of it, as always.

Wilipo grunted again.

That meant it was time to stop sparring. Nodding, Falco halted, breathing heavily. Ravi's reflexes were not as instantaneous and his fist clipped Falco.

Pain exploded in his head. *"Che diavolo!"*

The curse had spit from his mouth the moment Ravi struck, though Falco had no conscious knowledge of Italian. Or how he knew it was Italian. The intrigue saved Ravi from being pulverized.

Ravi bowed apologetically, dropping his hands to his sides. Rubbing his temples, Falco scowled over the late shot as a flash of memory spilled into his head.

White stucco. Glass. A house perched on a cliff, overlooking the ocean. *Malibu.* A warm breeze. A woman with red hair.

His house. He had a home, full of his things, his memories, his life.

The address scrolled through his mind as if it had always been there, along with images of street signs and impressions of direction, and he knew he could find it.

Home. He had to get there. Somehow.

One

At precisely 4:47 a.m., Caitlyn bolted awake, as she did every morning. The babies had started sleeping through the night, thank the good Lord, but despite that, their feeding time had ingrained itself into her body in some kind of whacked-out mommy alarm clock.

No one had warned her of that. Just as no one had warned her that triplets weren't three times the effort and nail-biting worry of one baby, but more like a zillion times.

But they also came with a zillion times the awe and adoration.

Caitlyn picked up the video monitor from her nightstand and watched her darlings sleep in their individual cribs. Antonio Junior sighed and flopped a fist back and forth as if he knew his mother was watching, but Leon and Annabelle slept like rocks. It was a genetic trait they shared with Vanessa, their biological mother, along with her red hair. Antonio had hair the color of a starless night, like his father.

And if he grew up to be half as hypnotically gorgeous as his father, she'd be beating the women off her son with a Louisville Slugger.

No matter how hard she tried, Caitlyn couldn't go back to sleep. Exhaustion was a condition she'd learned to live with and, maddeningly, it had nothing to do with how much sleep she got. Having fatherless eight-month-old triplets wreaked havoc on her sanity, and in the hours before dawn, all the questions and doubts and fears crowded into her mind.

Should she be doing more to meet an eligible man? Like what? Hang out in bars wearing a vomit-stained shirt, where she could chat up a few victims. "Hey, baby, have you ever fantasized about going all night long with triplets? Because I've got a proposition for you!"

No, the eligible men of Los Angeles were pretty safe from Caitlyn Hopewell, that was for sure. Even without the ready-made family, her relationship rules scared away most men: you didn't sleep with a man unless you were in love and there was a ring on your finger. Period. It was an absolute that had carried her through college and into adulthood, especially as she'd witnessed what passed for her sister Vanessa's criteria for getting naked with someone—he'd bought her jewelry or could get her further in her career. Caitlyn didn't want that for herself. And that pretty much guaranteed she'd stay single.

But how could she ever be enough for three children when, no matter how much she loved them, she wasn't supposed to be their mother? When she'd agreed to be Vanessa's surrogate, Caitlyn had planned on a nine-month commitment, not a lifetime. But fate had had different plans.

Caitlyn rolled from the king-size bed she still hadn't grown used to despite sleeping in it for over a year. Might as well get started on the day at—

she squinted at her phone—6:05 a.m. Threading her dark mess of curls through a ponytail holder, she threw on some yoga pants and a top, determined to get in at least twenty minutes of Pilates before Leon awoke.

She spread out her mat on the hardwood floor close to the glass wall overlooking the Malibu coastline, her favorite spot for tranquility. There was a full gym on the first floor of Antonio and Vanessa's mansion, but she couldn't bear to use it. Not yet. It had too much of Antonio stamped all over it, what with the mixed martial arts memorabilia hanging from the walls and the regulation ring in the center.

One day she'd clean it out, but as much as she hated the reminders of Antonio, she couldn't lose the priceless link to him. She hadn't removed any of Vanessa's things from the house, either, but had put a good bit away, where she couldn't see it every day.

Fifteen minutes later, her firstborn yowled through the monitor and Caitlyn dashed to the nursery across the hall from her bedroom before he woke up his brother and sister.

"There's my precious," she crooned and scooped up the gorgeous little bundle from his crib.

Like clockwork, he was always the first of the three to demand breakfast, and Caitlyn tried to spend alone time with each of her kids while feeding them. Brigitte, the babies' au pair, thought she was certifiable for breast-feeding triplets, but Caitlyn didn't mind. She loved bonding with the babies, and nobody ever saw her naked anyway; it was worth the potential hit to her figure to give the babies a leg up in the nutrition department.

The morning passed in a blur of babies and baths, and just as Caitlyn was about to return a phone call to her lawyer that she'd missed somewhere along the way, someone pounded on the front door.

Delivery guy, she hoped. She'd had to order a new car seat and it could not get here fast enough. Annabelle had christened hers in such a way that no bleach in existence could make it usable again and, honestly, Caitlyn had given up trying. There had to be some benefits to having custodial control of her children's billion-dollar inheritance.

"Brigitte? Can you get that?" Caitlyn called, but the girl didn't respond. Probably dealing with one of the kids, which was what she got paid well to do.

With a shrug, Caitlyn pocketed her phone and padded to the door, swinging it wide in full anticipation of a brown uniform–clad man.

It wasn't UPS. The unshaven man on her doorstep loomed over her, his dark gaze searching and familiar. There was something about the way he tilted his head—

"Antonio!" The strangled word barely made it past her throat as it seized up.

No! It couldn't be. Antonio had died in the same plane crash as Vanessa, over a year ago. Her brain fuzzed with disappointment, even as her heart latched on to the idea of her children's father standing before her in the flesh. Lack of sleep was catching up with her.

"Antonio," the man repeated and his eyes widened. "Do I know you?"

His raspy voice washed over her, turning inside her chest warmly, and tears pricked her eyelids. He even sounded like Antonio. She'd always loved his voice. "No, I don't think so. For a moment, I thought you were—"

A ghost. She choked it back.

His blank stare shouldn't have tripped her senses, but all at once, even with a full beard and weighing twenty pounds less, he looked so much like Antonio she couldn't stop greedily drinking him in.

"This is my house," he insisted firmly with a hint of wonderment as he glanced around the foyer beyond the open door. "I recognize it. But the Christmas tree is in the wrong place."

Automatically, she glanced behind her to note the location of the twelve-foot-high blue spruce she'd painstakingly arranged in the living room near the floor-to-ceiling glass wall facing the ocean.

"No, it's not," Caitlyn retorted.

Vanessa had always put the tree in the foyer so people could see it when they came in, but Caitlyn liked it by the sea. Then, every time you looked at the tree, you saw the water, too. Seemed logical to her, and this was her house now.

"I don't remember you." He cocked his head as if puzzled. "Did I sell you this house?"

She shook her head. "I...uh, live here with the owners."

The Malibu mansion was actually part of the

babies' estate. She hadn't wanted to move them from their parents' house and, according to the terms of Vanessa's and Antonio's wills, Caitlyn got to make all the decisions for the children.

"I remember a red-haired woman. Beautiful." His expression turned hard and slightly desperate. "Who is she?"

"Vanessa," Caitlyn responded without thinking. She shouldn't be so free with information. "Who are *you*?" she demanded.

"I don't know," he said between clenched teeth. "I remember flashes, incomplete pictures, and none of it makes sense. Tell me who I am."

Oh, my God. "You don't know who you are?" People didn't really get amnesia the way they did in movies. Did they?

Hand to her mouth, she evaluated this dirty, disheveled man wearing simple cotton pants rolled at the ankles and a torn cotton shirt. It couldn't be true. Antonio was dead.

If Antonio *wasn't* dead, where had he been since the plane crash? If he'd really lost his memory, it could explain why he'd been missing all this time.

But not why he'd suddenly shown up over a year later. Maybe he was one of those con men who preyed on grieving family members, and loss of memory was a convenient out to avoid incriminatory questions that would prove his identity, yet he couldn't answer.

But he'd known the Christmas tree was in the wrong place. What if he was telling the truth?

Her heart latched on to the idea and wouldn't let go.

Because— Oh, goodness. She'd always been half in love with her sister's husband and it all came rushing back. The guilt. The despondency at being passed over for the lush, gorgeous older Hopewell sister, the one who always got everything her heart desired. The covert sidelong glances at Antonio's profile during family dinners. Fantasies about what it would be like if he'd married her instead of Vanessa. The secret thrill at carrying Antonio's babies because Vanessa couldn't, and harboring secret dreams of Antonio falling at her feet, begging Caitlyn to be the mother of his children instead.

Okay, and she'd had a few secret dreams that involved some…carnal scenarios, like how Antonio's skin would feel against hers. What it would be like to kiss him. And love him in every sense of the word.

For the past six years, Caitlyn had lived with an almost biblical sense of shame, in a "thou shalt not covet thy sister's husband" kind of way. But she couldn't help it—Antonio had a wickedly sexy warrior's body and an enigmatic, watchful gaze that sliced through her when he turned it in her direction. Oh, she had it bad, and she'd never fully reconciled because it was intertwined with guilt—maybe she'd wished her sister ill and that was why the plane had crashed.

The guilt crushed down on her anew.

Tersely, he shook his head and that was when she noticed the scar bisecting his temple, which forked up into his dark, shaggy hair. On second thought, this man looked nothing like Antonio. With hard lines around his mouth, he was sharper, more angular, with shadows in his dark eyes that spoke of nightmares better left unexplained.

"I can't remem—you called me Antonio." Something vulnerable welled up in his gaze and then he winced. "Antonio Cavallari. Tell me. Is that my name?"

She hadn't mentioned Antonio's last name.

He could have learned the name of her children's father from anywhere. Los Angeles County tax records. From the millions of internet stories about the death of the former UFC champion and subsequent founder of the billion-dollar enterprise called Falco Fight Club after his career ended. Vanessa had had her own share of fame as an actress, playing the home-wrecking vixen everyone loved to hate on a popular nighttime drama. Her red hair had been part of her trademark look, and when she'd died, the internet had exploded with the news. Her sister's picture popped up now and again even a year later, so knowing about the color of Vanessa's hair wasn't terribly conclusive, either.

He could have pumped the next-door neighbor for information, for that matter.

Caitlyn refused to put her children in danger under any circumstances.

Sweeping him with a glance, she took as much of his measure as she could. But there was no calculation. No suggestion of shrewdness. Just confusion and a hint of the man who'd married her sister six years ago.

"Yes. Antonio Cavallari." Her eyelids fluttered

closed for a beat. What if she was wrong? What
if she just wanted him to be Antonio for all the
wrong reasons and became the victim of an elaborate fraud? Or worse—the victim of assault?

All at once, he sagged against the door frame,
babbling in a foreign language. Stricken, she
stared at him. She'd never heard Antonio speak
anything other than English.

Her stomach clenched. Blood tests. Dental records. Doctors' exams. There had to be a thousand ways to prove someone's identity. But what
was she supposed to do? Tell him to come back
with proof?

Then his face went white and he pitched to his
knees with a feeble curse, landing heavily on the
woven welcome mat.

It was a fitting condemnation. Welcoming, she
was not.

Throat tight with concern, she blurted out, "Are
you okay? What's wrong?"

"Tired. Hungry," he stated simply, eyes closed
and head lolling to one side. "I walked from the
docks."

"The docks?" Her eyes went wide. "The ones
near *Long Beach*? That's, like, fifty miles!"

"No identification," he said hoarsely. "No money."

The man couldn't even stand and, good grief, Caitlyn had certainly spent enough time in the company of actors to spot one—his weakened state was real.

"Come inside," she told him before she thought better of it. "Rest. And drink some water. Then we can sort this out."

It wasn't as if she was alone. Brigitte and Rosa, the housekeeper, were both upstairs. He might be Antonio, but that didn't make him automatically harmless, and who knew what his mental state was? But if he couldn't stand, he couldn't threaten anyone, let alone three women armed with cell phones and easy access to Francesco's top-dollar chef's knives.

He didn't even seem to register that she'd spoken, let alone acknowledge what he'd surely been after the whole time—an invitation inside. For a man who could be trying to scam her, he certainly wasn't chomping at the bit to gain entrance to her home.

Hesitating, she wondered if she should help him to his feet, but the thought of touching him had her hyperventilating. Either he was a strange man, or he was a most familiar one, and neither one gave her an ounce of comfort. Heat feathered across her cheeks as her chaste sensibilities warred with the practicality of helping someone in need.

He swayed and nearly toppled over, forcing her decision.

No way around it. She knelt and grabbed his arm, then slung it across her shoulders. The weight was strange and, oddly, a little exhilarating. The touch of a man was alien, though, no doubt—she hadn't gone on a date in over two years. Her mind went blank as he slumped against her.

Looping her own arm around his waist, she pushed up with her legs, grateful for the core strength she'd developed through rigorous Pilates, both before and after the babies were born.

Gracious. He smelled like three-day-old fish and other pungencies she hesitated to identify— and she'd have sworn babies produced the worst stench in the world.

The man hobbled along with her across the threshold, thankfully revived enough to do so under his own power. When she paused in front of the pristine eggshell-colored suede sofa in the formal living area, he immediately dropped vertically onto the cushions without hesitation. Groaning, he covered his eyes with his arm.

"Water," he murmured and lay still as death.

And now for the second dilemma. Leave him unattended while she fetched a glassful from the wet bar across the foyer in Antonio's study? It wasn't that far, and she was being silly worrying about a near comatose man posing some sort of threat. She dashed across the marble at breakneck pace, filled the glass at the small stainless-steel sink and dashed back without spilling it, thankfully.

"Here it is," she said to alert him she'd returned.

The arm over his eyes moved up, sweeping the long, shaggy mane away from his forehead. Blearily he peered at her through bloodshot eyes, and without the hair obscuring his face, he looked totally different. Exactly like Antonio, the man she'd secretly studied, pined over, fantasized about for years. She gasped.

"I won't hurt you," he muttered as he sat up,

pain etching deeper lines into his face. "Just want water."

She handed it to him, unable to tear her gaze from his face, even as chunks of matted hair fell back over his forehead. Regardless of her immense guilt over his presumed identity, she couldn't go on arguing with herself over it. There was one way to settle this matter right now.

"Do you think you're Antonio?" she asked as he drank deeply from the glass.

"I..." He glanced up at her, his gaze full of emotions she couldn't name, but those dark, mysterious eyes held her captive. "I don't remember. That's why I'm here. I want to know."

"There's one way." Before she lost her courage, she pointed to her chest over her heart as her pulse raced at the promise. "Antonio has a rather elaborate tattoo. Right here. Do you?"

It wouldn't be impossible to replicate. But difficult, as the tattoo had been commissioned by a famous artist who had a unique tribal style.

Without breaking eye contact, he set his water glass on the side table and unbuttoned his shirt to midchest. *Unbuttoned his shirt*, as if they were intimate and she had every right to see him unclothed.

"It says Falco. What does it mean?" he asked.

The truth washed through her even before he drew his shirt aside to reveal the red-and-black falcon screaming across his pectoral muscle. Her gaze locked on to the ink, registering the chiseled flesh beneath it, and it kicked at her way down low with a long, hot pull, exactly the way she'd always reacted to Antonio.

She blinked and refocused on his face. The sight of his cut, athletic torso—sun browned and more enthralling than she'd ever have expected—wouldn't fade from her mind.

That tattoo had always been an electrifying aspect of his dangerous appeal. And, oh, my—it still was.

"It means that's proof enough for me to know you're Antonio." She shut her eyes, unable to process the relief flooding through his gaze. Unable to process the sharp thrill in her midsection that was wholly erotic...and felt an awful lot like trouble. Stunning, resplendent, *forbidden* Antonio Cavallari was alive. "And we have a lot of hurdles in front of us."

Everything in her world had just slid off a cliff.

The long, legal nightmare of the past year as she'd fought for her right to the babies had been for nothing. Nearly two years ago, she'd signed a surrogacy agreement, but then a year ago Vanessa and Antonio had crashed into the South China Sea. After months of court appearances, a judge had finally overturned the rights she'd signed away and given her full custody of her children.

Oh, dear Lord. This was Antonio's home. It was his money. *Her children were his.* And he had every right to take them away from her.

Two

Antonio—he rolled the name around on his tongue, and it didn't feel wrong like Falco had. Before Indonesia, he'd been called both Antonio and Falco by blurry-faced people, some with cameras, some with serious expressions as they spoke to him about important matters. A crowd had chanted *Falco* like a tribal drum, bouncing off the ceiling of a huge, cavernous arena.

The headache nearly flattened him again, as it always did when he tried too hard to force open his mind.

Instead, he contemplated the blushing, dark-haired and very attractive woman who seemed vaguely familiar but not enough to place her. She didn't belong in his house. She shouldn't be living here, but he had no clue where that sense came from. "What is your name?"

"Caitlyn. Hopewell," she added in what appeared to be an afterthought. "Vanessa is— was—my sister." She eyed him. "You remember Vanessa but not me?"

"The redhead?" At Caitlyn's nod, he frowned.

No, he didn't remember Vanessa, not the way he remembered his house. A woman with flame-colored hair haunted his dreams. Bits and pieces floated through his mind. The images were laced with flashes of her flesh as if he'd often seen her naked, but her face wouldn't quite clarify, as though he'd created an impressionist painting of this woman whose name he couldn't recall.

Frustration rose again. Because how was it fair that he knew exactly what an impressionist painting was but not who *he* was?

After Ravi had knocked loose the memories of his house, Antonio had left Indonesia the next morning, hopping fishing boats and stowing away amidst heavy cargo containers for days and days, all to reach Los Angeles in hopes of regaining more precious links with his past.

This delicate, ethereally beautiful woman—Caitlyn—held a few of these keys, and he needed her to provide them. "Who is Vanessa to me?"

"Your wife," she announced softly. "You didn't know that?"

He shook his head. Married. He was *married* to Vanessa? It was an entire piece of his life, his persona, he'd had no idea existed. Had he been in love with her? Had his wife looked for him at all, distraught over his fate, or just written him off when he went missing?

Would he even recognize Vanessa if she stood before him?

Glancing around the living room for which he'd instantly and distinctly recalled purchasing the furnishings—without the help of anyone, let alone the red-haired woman teasing the edges of his memory—he asked, "Where is she?"

"She died." Grief welled up across her classical features. The sisters must have been close, which was probably why Caitlyn seemed familiar. "You were both involved in the same plane crash shortly after leaving Thailand."

"Plane crash?" The wispy images of the red-

haired woman vanished as he zeroed in on Caitlyn. "Is that what happened?"

Thailand. He'd visited Thailand—but never
made it home. Until now.

Eyes bright with unshed tears, she nodded, dark
ponytail flipping over her shoulder. "Over a year
ago."

All at once, he wanted to mourn for this wife
he couldn't remember. Because it would mean he
could still experience emotions that stayed maddeningly out of reach, emotions with clinical def-
initions—love, peace, happiness, fulfillment, the
list went on and on—but which had no real context. He wanted to feel *something* other than dis-
couraged and adrift.

His head ached, but he pressed on, determined
to unearth more clues to how he'd started out on
a plane from Thailand and ended up in a fishing
village in Indonesia. Alone. "But I was on the
plane. And I'm not dead. Maybe Vanessa is still
alive, too."

Her name produced a small ping in his heart,
but he couldn't be certain if the feeling lingered
from before the crash or if he'd manufactured it
out of his intense need to remember.

Hand to her mouth, Caitlyn bowed her head. "No. They recovered her…body," she murmured, her voice thick. "They found the majority of the fuselage in the water. Most of the forty-seven people on board were still in their seats."

Vivid, gory images spilled into his mind as he imagined the horrors his wife—and the rest of the passengers—must have gone through before succumbing to the death he'd escaped.

"Except me."

For the first time, his reality felt a bit like a miracle instead of a punishment. How had he escaped? Had he unbuckled himself in time to avoid drowning or had he been thrown free of the wreckage?

"Except you," she agreed, though apparently it had taken the revelation of his strange falcon tattoo to convince her. "And two other passengers, who were sitting across the aisle from you in first class. You were all in the first row, including Vanessa. They searched for survivors for a week, but there was no trace."

"They were looking in the wrong place," he growled. "I washed up on the beach in Indonesia. On the south side of Batam Island."

"I don't know my geography, but the plane crashed into the ocean near the coast of Malaysia. That's where they focused the search."

No wonder no one had found him. They'd been hundreds of miles off.

"After a month," she continued, "they declared all three of you dead."

But he wasn't dead.

The other two passengers might have survived, as well. *Look for them.* They might be suffering from memory loss or ghastly injuries. They might be frightened and alone, having clawed their way out of a watery crypt, only to face a fully awake nightmare. As he had.

He had to find them. But he had no money, no resources—not at this moment anyway. He must have money, or at least he must have had some once. The sum he'd paid for this house popped into his head out of nowhere: fifteen point eight million dollars. That had been eight years ago.

Groaning, he rubbed his temples as the headache grew uncontrollable.

"Are you okay?" Caitlyn asked.

Ensuring the comfort of others seemed to come naturally to this woman he'd found living in his house. His sister-in-law. Had she always been so nurturing?

"Fine," he said between clenched teeth. "Is this still my house?"

He could sell it and use the proceeds to live on while he combed the South China Sea.

Caitlyn chose that moment to sit next to him on the couch, overwhelming him with the light scent of coconut, which, strangely, made him want to bury his nose in her hair.

"Technically, no. When you were declared dead, it passed to your heirs."

"You mean Vanessa's?" Seemed as if his wife's sister had made out pretty well after the plane crash. "Are you the only heir? Because I'm not dead and I want my money back."

It was the only way he could launch a search for the other two missing passengers.

"Oh." She stared at him, her sea-glass-blue eyes wide with guilt and a myriad of other emotions he suddenly wished to understand.

Because looking into her eyes made him feel something. Something good and beautiful and he didn't want to stop drowning in her gaze.

"You don't remember, do you?" she asked. "Oh,

my gosh. I've been rambling and you don't even know about the babies."

Blood rushed from his head so fast, his ears popped.

"Babies?" he croaked. Surely she didn't mean babies, plural, as in more than one? As in *his* babies?

"Triplets." She shot him a misty smile that heightened her ethereal beauty. Which he wished he could appreciate, but there was no way, not with the bomb she'd just dropped. "And by some miracle, they still have a father. You. Would you like to meet them?"

"I…" A father. He had children? Three of them, apparently. "They're really mine?" Stupid question, but this was beyond—he shook his head. "How old are they? Do they remember me?"

"Oh, no, they weren't born yet when you went to Thailand."

He frowned. "But you said Vanessa died in the plane crash. Is she not their mother?"

Had he cheated on his wife with another woman? Catholic-school lessons from his youth blasted through his mind instantly. Infidelity was wrong.

"She's not," Caitlyn refuted definitively. "I am."

Guilt and shame cramped his gut as he eyed Caitlyn. He'd cheated on his wife with his *sister-in-law*? The thought was reprehensible.

But it explained the instant visceral reaction he had to her.

Her delicate, refined beauty didn't match the obvious lushness of the redhead he'd married. Maybe that was the point. He really preferred a dark-haired, more classically attractive woman like Caitlyn if he'd fathered children with her.

"Were we having an affair?" he asked bluntly. And would he have a serious fight to regain control of his money now that his mistress had her hooks into it?

Pink spread across her cheeks in a gorgeous blush, and a foreign heaviness filled his chest, spreading to heat his lower half. Though he couldn't recall having made love to her before, he had no trouble recognizing the raw, carnal attraction to Caitlyn. Obviously, she was precisely the woman he preferred, judging by his body's unfiltered reaction.

"Of course not!" She wouldn't meet his gaze, and her blush deepened. "You were married to my sister and I would never—well, I mean, I did meet you first and, okay, maybe I thought about… but then I introduced you to Vanessa. That was that. You were hers. Not that I blame you—"

"Caitlyn."

Her name alone caused that strange fullness in his chest. He'd like to say it again. Whisper it to her as he learned what she tasted like.

She glanced up, finally silenced, and he would very much like to understand why her self-conscious babbling had caused the corners of his mouth to turn up. It was evident from the way she nervously twisted her fingers together that she had no concept of how to lie. They'd never been involved. He'd stake his life on it.

He cleared his raspy throat. "How did the children come to be, then?"

"Oh. I was your surrogate. Yours and Vanessa's. The children are a hundred percent your DNA, grown in my womb." She wrinkled her nose. "That sounds so scientific. Vanessa couldn't conceive, so I volunteered to carry the baby. Granted, I didn't know three eggs were going to take."

She laughed and he somehow found the energy

to be charmed by her light spirit. "So Vanessa and I, we were happy?"

If only he could remember her. Remember if they'd laughed together as he vaguely sensed that lovers should. Had they dreamed together of the babies on the way, planning for their family? Had she cried out in her last moments, grief stricken that she'd never hold her children?

"Madly in love." Caitlyn sighed happily. "It was a grand story. Falco and the Vixen. The media adored you guys. I'll go ask Brigitte, the au pair, to bring down the babies."

Reality overwhelmed him.

"Wait." Panicked all of a sudden, he clamped down on her arm before she could rise. "I can't… They don't know me."

He was a father. But so far from a father, he couldn't fathom the idea of three helpless infants under his care. What if he broke one? What if he scared them? How did you handle a baby? How did you handle *three*?

"Five minutes," she said calmly. "Say hello. See them and count their fingers and toes. Then I'll have Brigitte take them away. They'll get used to you, I promise."

But would he get used to them? "Five minutes. And then I'd like to clean up. Eat."

Breathe. Get his bearings. Figure out how to be Antonio Cavallari again before he had to figure out how to be Antonio Cavallari plus three.

"Of course. I'm sorry, I should have thought of that." Dismay curved her mouth downward.

"There is no protocol when the dead come back to life," he countered drily and smiled. Apparently he'd found a sense of humor along with his home.

His head spun as Caitlyn disappeared upstairs to retrieve the babies and Brigitte, whoever that was. A few minutes later, she returned, followed by a young blonde girl pushing a three-seated carriage. Everything faded away as he saw his children.

Three little heads rested against the cushions, with three sets of eyes and three mouths. Wonder and awe crushed his heart as he drank in the sight of these creatures he'd had a hand in creating.

"They're really mine?" he whispered.

"Really, really," Caitlyn confirmed at normal volume, her tone slightly amused.

She picked up the one from the first seat and

held him in the crook of her arm, angling the baby to face him. The blue outfit meant this was his son, didn't it?

"This is Leon." Her mouth quirked. "He's named after my father. I guess it's too late to ask if that's okay, but I thought it was a nice tribute to Vanessa's role in his heritage."

"It's fine."

Antonio was still whispering, but his voice caught in his throat and he couldn't have uttered another sound as his son mewled like a hungry cat, his gaze sharp and bright as he cocked his head as if contemplating the secrets of the universe.

His son. Leon.

Such a simple concept, procreating. People did it every day in all corners of the world. Wilipo had fourteen children and as far as Antonio could tell, never thought it particularly miraculous.

But it *was*.

This little person with the short baby-fine red hair was his child.

"You can say hello," Caitlyn reminded him.

"Hello." His son didn't acknowledge that Antonio had spoken, preferring to bury his head in

Caitlyn's shoulder. Had he said the wrong thing? Maybe his voice was too scratchy.

"He'll warm up, I promise." She slid Leon back into the baby seat and picked up the next one.

The pink outfit filled his vision and stung his eyes. He had a daughter. The heart he could have sworn was already full of his son grew so big, he was shocked it hadn't burst from his rib cage.

"This is Annabelle. I always wanted to have a daughter named Annabelle," Caitlyn informed him casually, as if they were discussing the weather instead of this little bundle of perfection.

"She has red hair, too," he murmured. "Like her brother."

Her beautiful face turned up at the sound of his voice and he got lost in her blue eyes.

He had a very bad feeling that the word *no* had just vanished from his vocabulary, and he looked forward to spoiling his daughter to the point of ridiculousness.

"Yes, she and Leon take after Vanessa. Which means Annabelle will be a knockout by the time she's fourteen. Be warned," she said wryly with a half laugh.

"I know martial arts," he muttered. "Any

smarmy Romeo with illicit intentions will find himself minus a spleen if he touches my daughter."

Caitlyn smirked. "I don't think a male on the planet would come within fifty yards of Annabelle if they knew you were her father. I was warning you about *her.*"

With that cryptic comment, she spirited away his daughter far too quickly and replaced her with the third baby, clad in blue.

"This is Antonio Junior," Caitlyn said quietly and moved closer to present his other son. "He looks just like you, don't you think?"

Dark hair capped a serious face with dark eyes. Antonio studied this third child and his gut lurched with an unnatural sense of recognition, as if the missing pieces of his soul had been snapped into place to form this tiny person.

"Yes," he whispered.

And suddenly, his new lease on life had a purpose.

When he'd set off from Indonesia to find his past, he'd never dreamed he'd instead find his future. A tragic plane crash had nearly robbed these three innocent lives of both their parents, but against all odds, Antonio had survived.

Now he knew why. So he could be a father.

* * *

As promised, Caitlyn rounded up the babies and sent them upstairs with Brigitte so Antonio could decompress. Brigitte, bless her, didn't ask any more questions about Antonio's presence, but Caitlyn could tell her hurried explanation that he'd been ill and unable to travel home hadn't satisfied the au pair. Neither would it be enough for the hordes of media and legal hounds who would be snapping at their heels soon enough.

The amazing return of Antonio Cavallari would make worldwide headlines, of that she was sure. But first, he needed to rest and then see a discreet doctor. The world didn't have to know right away. The household staff had signed nondisclosure agreements, and in Hollywood, that was taken so seriously, none of them would ever work again if they broke it. So Caitlyn felt fairly confident the few people who knew about the situation would keep quiet.

She showed him to the master suite, glad now that she'd never cleaned it out, though she'd have to get Rosa to pack up Vanessa's things. It was too morbid to expect him to use his former bedroom with his late wife's clothes still in the dresser.

"I'll send Rosa, the housekeeper, up with something to eat," she promised and left him to clean up.

She wandered to the sunroom and pretended to read a book about parenting multiples on her e-reader, but she couldn't clear the jagged emotion from her throat. Antonio's face when he'd met his children for the first time... It had been amazing to see that much love crowd into his expression instantly. She wished he could have been there in the delivery room, to hold her hand and smile at her like that. Tell her everything would be okay and he'd still think she was beautiful even with a C-section scar.

Except if he *had* been there, he'd have held Vanessa's hand, not hers, and the reality squelched Caitlyn's little daydream.

The babies were his. It wouldn't take long for a judge to overturn her custody rights, not when she'd signed a surrogacy agreement that stated she'd have no claim over the babies once they were born.

But the babies were hers, too. The hospital had listed her name on their birth certificates as their mother—who else would they have named? She'd been their sole parent for nearly eight months and before that, carried them in her womb for months, knowing they weren't going home with Vanessa and Antonio as planned, but with her.

It was a mess, and more than anything, she wanted to do what was best for the babies. Not for the first time, she wished her mother was still alive; Caitlyn could use some advice.

An hour later, Antonio reappeared.

He filled the doorway of the sunroom and the late-afternoon rays highlighted his form with an otherworldly glow that revealed the true nature of his return to this realm—as that of an angel.

She gasped, hand flying to her mouth.

Then he moved into the room and became flesh and blood once again. But no less beautiful.

He'd trimmed his full beard, revealing his deep cheekbones and allowing his arresting eyes to become the focal point of his face. He'd swept back his still long midnight-colored hair and dressed in his old clothes, which didn't fit nearly as well as they once had, but a man as devastatingly handsome as Antonio could make a bedsheet draped over his body work.

Heat swept along her cheeks as she imagined

exactly that, and it did not resemble the toga she'd meant to envision. *Antonio, spread out on the bed, sheet barely covering his sinewy, drool-worthy fighter's physique, gaze dark and full of desire...for her...* She shook her head. That was the *last* thing she should be thinking about for a hundred reasons, but Antonio Junior, Leon and Annabelle were the top three and she needed to get a few things straight with their father. No naked masculine chests required for that conversation.

"You look...different," she squawked.

Nice. *Tip him off that you're thinking naughty thoughts.*

"You kept my clothes?" He pointed to the jeans slung low on his lean hips. "And my shaving equipment?"

All of which he apparently remembered just fine as he'd slipped back into his precrash look easily. Antonio had always been gorgeous as sin, built like a lost Michelangelo sculpture with a side of raw, masculine power. And she was still salivating over him. A year in Indonesia hadn't changed that, apparently.

She shrugged and tried to make herself stop

staring at him, which didn't exactly work. "I kept meaning to go through that room, but I thought maybe there would be something the babies would want. So I left it."

"I'm glad you did. Thank you." His small smile tripped a long liquid pull inside and she tamped it down. Or she almost did. It was too delicious to fully let it go.

Serious. Talk. Now, she told herself sternly.

"I had a gym," he said before she could work up the courage to bring up item one on her long list of issues. "Did you leave it alone, too?"

"It's untouched."

"I need to see it. Will you come with me?"

Surprised, she nodded. "Of course."

Was it wrong to be thrilled he'd asked her to be with him as he delved into his past?

Well, if that was wrong, it was probably just as wrong to still have a thing for him all these years later. If only she hadn't given up so easily when she'd first met him—it was still one of her biggest regrets.

But then, her relationship rules didn't afford much hope unless a man was interested enough to hang around for the long haul. She'd thought maybe Antonio might have been, once upon a time. The way he'd flirted with her when they'd met, as though he thought she was beautiful, had floored her...and then Vanessa had entered stage left, which had dried up his interest in the chaste sister.

She followed him as he strolled directly to the gym, mystified how he remembered the way, and halted next to him as he quietly took in the posters advertising his many fights, his championship belts and publicity shots of himself clad in shorts and striking a fierce pose.

There was something wicked about staring at a photo of Antonio half clothed while standing next to the fully dressed version, knowing that falcon tattoo sat under his shirt, waiting to be discovered by a woman's fingers. *Her* fingers. What would it feel like?

Sometimes she dreamed about that.

"Do you remember any of this?" she asked as the silence stretched. She couldn't keep thinking about Antonio's naked chest. Which became more difficult the longer they stood there, his heat nearly palpable. He even smelled like sin.

"Bits and pieces," he finally said. "I didn't

know I had martial arts training. I thought I was remembering a movie, because I wasn't always in the ring. Sometimes I was outside the ring, watching."

"Oh, like watching other fighters? Maybe you're remembering Falco," she offered. "The fight club."

He shook his head as if to clear it. "I feel as if I should know what that is."

He didn't remember Falco, either? Antonio had lived and breathed that place, much to Vanessa's dismay on many occasions. Her sister had hoped to see her husband more often once his time in the ring was up, but the opposite had proved true.

Caitlyn led him to a picture on the wall, the one of him standing with two fighters about to enter the ring. "Falco is your MMA promotional venue. You founded it once your career ended. That's where you made all your money."

"When did I stop fighting?"

"It wasn't long after you and Vanessa got married. You don't remember that, either?" When he shook his head, she told him what little she knew about his last fight. "Brian Kerr nearly killed you. Illegal punch to the back of your head and you hit the floor at a bad angle. Knocked you out. You were in the hospital unconscious for two days. That's probably why your amnesia is so pronounced. Your brain has sustained quite a bit of trauma."

Really, he should have already been checked out by a competent doctor, but he'd refused when she'd mentioned it earlier. It wasn't as if she could make him. Caitlyn had no experience with amnesia *or* a powerful man who wouldn't admit to weakness.

Deep down, she had an undeniable desire to gain some experience, especially since it came wrapped in an Antonio package.

He stared at the picture for a moment. "Falco is the name of my company," he announced cautiously as if testing it out. "It's not *my* name."

Her heart ached over his obvious confusion. She wanted to help him, to erase that small bit of helplessness she would never have associated with confident, solid Antonio Cavallari if she hadn't seen it firsthand.

"Falco was your nickname when you were fighting. You transferred it to your promotional company because I guess it had some sentimental value." Not that he'd ever discussed it with her. It was an assumption everyone had made, regardless.

"What happened to my company while I was missing?"

Missing—was that how he'd thought of himself? She tried to put herself in his place, waking up with few memories, in a strange place, with strange people who spoke a different language, all while recuperating from a plane crash and near drowning. The picture was not pretty, which tugged at her heart anew.

"I, um, have control over it." And it had languished like the bedroom and his gym.

What did she know about running an MMA promotional company? But she couldn't have sold it or tried to step into his shoes. In many ways, his place in the world had been on accidental hold, as if a higher power had stilled her hand from dismantling Antonio's life. It had been here, waiting for him to slip back into it.

His expression hardened and the glimpse of vulnerability vanished. "I want control of my estate. And my company. Do whatever you have to do to make that happen."

The rasp in his voice, which hadn't been there before he got on that plane, laced his statement with a menacing undertone. He seemed more like a stranger in that moment than he had when he'd first appeared on her doorstep, unkempt and un-recognizable.

It was a brutal reminder that he wasn't the same man. He wasn't a safe fantasy come to life. And she wasn't her sister, a woman who could easily handle a man like Antonio—worse, she wasn't the woman he'd picked.

"It's a lot to process, I realize," she said slowly as her pulse skittered out of control. This harder, hooded Antonio was impossible to read, and she had no idea how to handle this unprecedented sit-uation. "But you just got back to the States. You don't even remember Falco, let alone how to run it. Why don't you take a few days, get your bear-ings? I'll help you."

The offer was genuine. But it also kept her in his proximity so she could figure out his plans. If she got a hint that he was thinking about fight-ing her for custody of the triplets, she'd be ready.

She was their mother, and this man—who was still very much a ghost of his former self—was not taking away her children.

Three

Antonio shifted his iron-hard gaze from the pictures on the wall to evaluate Caitlyn coolly, which did not help her pulse. Nothing in her limited experience had prepared her to face down a man like Antonio, but she had to make him agree to a few ground rules.

"You cannot fathom what I've been through over the past year," he stated firmly. "I want nothing more than to pick up the pieces of my life and begin the next chapter with these new cards I've been dealt. I need my identity back."

Which was a perfectly reasonable request, but executing it more closely resembled unsnarling a knotted skein of yarn than simply handing over a few account numbers. This was one time when she couldn't afford to back down.

Caitlyn nodded and took a deep breath. "I understand, and I'm not suggesting otherwise. The problem is that a lot of legalities are involved and I have to look out for the interests of the children."

His gaze softened, warming her, and she didn't know what to do with that, either.

"I'm thinking of the children, as well."

"Good. Then, it would be best to take things slowly. You've been gone for a long time and the babies have a routine. It would be catastrophic to disrupt them."

He pursed his lips. "If you're concerned that I might dismiss the nanny, I can assure you I have no intention of doing so. I couldn't care for one child by myself, let alone three."

Her stomach jolted and she swallowed, gearing up to lay it on the line. "You won't be by yourself. I'll still be here."

If only her voice hadn't squeaked, that might have come across more definitively. Besides, she was still breast-feeding and didn't plan to stop until the triplets were a year old. She was irreplaceable, as far as she was concerned.

"You're free to get back to your life," he said with a puzzled frown. "There's no reason for you to continue in your role as caretaker now that I've returned."

"Whoa." She threw up a palm as the back of her neck heated in a sweaty combination of anger and fear. "Where did you get the idea that I'm just a caretaker? The babies are *mine*. I'm their mother."

Nothing she'd said thus far had sunk in, obviously.

Antonio crossed his arms and contemplated her. "You said you were the surrogate. A huge sacrifice, to be sure, but the children would have been mine and Vanessa's. You've been forced to care for them much longer than anyone has a right to ask. I'm relieving you of the responsibility."

Her worst nightmare roared to life, pulsing and seething as it went for her jugular.

"No!" A tear rolled down her face before she could stop it as she tried to summon up a reasonable argument against the truth in his words. "That's not what happened. I care for them because I love them. They became mine in every sense when I thought you and Vanessa were both gone. I *need* them. And they need me. Don't take away my babies."

A sob choked off whatever else she'd been about to say. The one and only time she'd ever tried to fight for something, and instead of using logic and reason, she'd turned into an emotional mess.

Concern weighted Antonio's expression as he reached out to grasp her hand in a totally surprising move. His fingers found hers and squeezed tightly, shooting an unexpected thrill through her that she couldn't contain. Coupled with the emotional distress, it was almost overwhelming.

"Don't cry." The lines around his eyes deepened as he heaved a ragged sigh. "I don't know how to do this."

"But you don't have to know," she countered, clinging to his hand like a lifeline. "That's what I'm trying to tell you. Don't change anything. It's Christmastime and we're family, if nothing else. I'll stay here and continue to care for the babies, then we can spend this time figuring it out together. After the first of the year, maybe the path will seem clearer."

Please, God.

Relief coursed through her as he slowly nodded.

"I want to be as fair as possible to everyone. If you don't have a life to get back to, then it makes sense for you to stay here. At least until January."

"This *is* my life."

Or at least it was now, since she'd given up her job as an accountant. She had no desire to be anything other than the mother she'd become over the past year. And now she had until the first of January to find a way to stay in that role. If Antonio decided his children would be better off in another arrangement, she had little to say about it.

What would she do without the family she'd formed?

"Caitlyn, I appreciate what you've done." His dark eyes sought hers and held, his gratitude genuine. "You stepped into my place to care for my children. Thank you."

That he recognized her efforts meant the world to her. He was a good man, deep inside where brain trauma couldn't touch. As she'd always known.

She nodded, still too emotional to respond, but the sentiment gave her hope. He wasn't heartless, just trying to do the right thing.

Somehow, Antonio had to recognize that *she*

was the right thing for the children and then the two of them could figure out how to be co-parents. After learning how to handle triplets, that should be a walk in the park.

The next two days passed in a blur. When Caitlyn had mentioned legalities, Antonio had half thought it was an excuse to avoid giving up control of his money. But she'd vastly understated the actuality. An avalanche of paperwork awaited him once the man who'd been his lawyer for a decade became convinced Antonio had really returned from the dead.

Funny how he'd instantly recognized Kyle Lowery the moment his lawyer's admin had ushered Antonio and Caitlyn into the man's office. His memory problems were inconsistent and frustrating, to say the least.

Antonio's headache persisted and grew worse the more documents Kyle's paralegal placed in front of him. The harsh lights glinting from the gold balls on the Christmas tree in the corner didn't help. Antonio wished he could enjoy the spirit of the season.

But Christmas and family and all of the joy

others seemed to associate with this time of year meant little to him. Caitlyn had told him that his parents had died some time back, which probably explained why he remembered them with a sense of distance, as if the scenes had happened long ago.

After many more stops and an interminable number of hours, he had: a temporary driver's license, a temporary bank card, a promise of credit cards to come, a bank teller who'd fallen all over herself to give him access to his safe-deposit box…and a dark-haired enigma of a woman who'd stuck to his side like glue, determined to help him navigate the exhausting quagmire re-entering his life had become.

Why was she still here?

Why did her presence make him so happy? She somehow made everything better just by being near him. And sometimes, she looked at him a certain way that burrowed under his skin with tingly warmth. Both had become necessary. Unexpectedly so.

He studied her covertly at lunch on the third day after he'd pounded on the door of his Malibu house, delirious and determined to find answers to the question marks in his mind.

What he'd found still hadn't fully registered. Caitlyn was an amazing woman and his kids were surprising, funny little people. Together, they were a potent package. But how did that make sense? She wasn't their biological mother.

While Antonio absently chewed on a thick sandwich designed to put back some of his lost weight, Caitlyn laughed at Leon as he shoved his food off his tray to the floor below.

She'd insisted on the triplets sitting at the table when the adults had meals, even though the babies ate little more than puree of something and bits of Cheerios. Antonio wouldn't have thought of having infants join them, but with the additions, eating became something more than a routine. It was a chance to spend time with his children without expectation since Brigitte and Caitlyn handled everything.

Secretly, he was grateful Caitlyn hadn't skipped through the door the moment he'd given her the out. In the hazy reaches of his mind, he had the distinct impression most women would have run very fast in the other direction from triplets. He couldn't understand Caitlyn's motivation for staying unless she thought she'd get a chunk of his estate as a thank-you. Which he'd probably give her. She deserved something for her sacrifices.

"Your turn."

Antonio did a double take at the spoon in Caitlyn's outstretched hand and blinked. "My turn to what?"

"Feed your daughter. She won't bite you." Caitlyn raised her brows and nodded at the spoon. "Of the three, Annabelle is the most laid-back about eating, so start with her."

Since he couldn't see a graceful way to refuse, he accepted the spoon and scooted closer to the baby's high chair, eyeing the bowl of...whatever it was. Orange applesauce?

Scowling, he scooped some up and then squinted at the baby watching him with bright eyes. How was he supposed to feed her with her fingers stuck in her mouth?

"Come on, open," he commanded.

Annabelle fluttered her lashes and made an uncomplimentary noise, fingers firmly wedged where the spoon was supposed to go.

He tried again. "Please?"

Caitlyn giggled and he glanced at her askance, which only made her laugh harder. He rolled his shoulders, determined to pass this one small test, but getting his daughter to eat might top the list of the most difficult things he had to do today.

Antonio had learned to walk again on the poorly healed broken leg that the Indonesian doctor had promised would have to be amputated. He'd defied the odds and scarcely even had a limp now. If he could do that, one very small person could not break him.

He tapped the back of Annabelle's hand with the edge of the spoon, hoping that would act as an open sesame, but she picked that moment to yank her fingers free. She backhanded the spoon, flinging it free of Antonio's grip. It hit the wall with a *thunk*, leaving a splash of orange in a trail to the floor.

Frustration welled. He balled his fists automatically and then immediately shoved them into his lap as horror filtered through him. His first instinct was to fight, but he had to control that impulse, or else what kind of father was he going to be?

Breathing rhythmically, he willed back the frustration until his fists loosened. Better.

His first foray into caring for his kid and she elected to show him her best defensive moves. Annabelle blinked innocently as Antonio's scowl deepened. "Yeah, you work on that technique, and when you've got your spinning backhand down, we'll talk."

Spinning backhand. The phrase had leaped into his mind with no forethought. Instantly other techniques scrolled through his head. *Muay Thai.* That had been his specialty. His "training" with Wilipo had come so easily because Antonio should have been teaching the class as the master, not attending as the student.

Faster now, ingrained drills, disciplines and defense strategies exploded in his mind. Why now instead of in his gym, surrounded by the relics of his former status as a mixed martial arts champion?

The headache slammed him harder than ever before and the groan escaped before he could catch it.

"It's okay," Caitlyn said and jumped up to retrieve the spoon. "You don't have to feed her. I just thought you might like it."

"No problem," he said around the splitting pain in his temples. "Excuse me."

He mounted the stairs to his bedroom and shut himself away in the darkened room, but refused to lie on the bed like an invalid.

Instead, he sank into a chair and put his head in his hands. This couldn't go on, the rush of memories and the headaches and the inability to do simple tasks like stick a spoon in a baby's mouth without becoming irrational.

But how did he change it?

Coming to LA was supposed to solve everything, give him back his memories and his life. It had only highlighted how very far he had yet to go in his journey back to the land of the living.

An hour later, the pain was manageable enough to try being civilized again. Antonio tracked down Caitlyn in the sunroom, which seemed to be her favored spot when she wasn't hanging out with the babies. Her dark curls partially obscured the e-reader in her hands and she seemed absorbed in the words on the screen.

"I'll visit a doctor," he told her shortly and

spun to leave before she asked any questions. She'd been after him to see one, but he'd thus far refused, having had enough of the medical profession during his months and months of rehabilitation in Indonesia.

No doctor could restore his memories, nor could one erase the scars he bore from the plane crash.

But if a Western doctor had a way to make his headaches go away, that would be stellar. He had to become a father, one way or another, and living in a crippling state of pain wasn't going to cut it.

"I'll drive you." She followed him into the hall. "Just because you have a driver's license doesn't mean you're ready to get behind the wheel. We'll take my—"

"Caitlyn." He whirled to face her, but she kept going, smacking into his chest.

His arms came up as they both nearly lost their balance and somehow she ended up pinned to the wall, their bodies tangled and flush. His lower half sprang to attention and heat shot through his gut.

Caitlyn's wide-eyed gaze captured his and he couldn't have broken the connection if his life depended on it. Her chest heaved against his as if she was unable to catch her breath, and that excited him, too.

"Caitlyn," he murmured again, but that seemed to be the extent of his ability to speak as her lips parted, drawing his attention to her mouth. She caught her plump bottom lip between her teeth and—

"Um, you can let go now," she said and cleared her throat. "I'm okay."

He released her, stepping back to allow her the space she'd asked for, though it was far from what he wanted to do. "I'm curious about something."

Nervously, she rearranged her glossy hair, refusing to meet his eyes. "Sure."

"You said that you introduced me to Vanessa. How did you and I meet?" Because if he'd ever held Caitlyn in his arms before, he was an idiot if he'd willingly let her go.

"I was Rick's accountant." At his raised brows, she smiled. "Your former manager. He'd gone through several CPAs until he found me, and when I came by his house to do his quarterly taxes, you were there. You were wearing a pink shirt for a breast cancer fund-raiser you'd attended. We got to talking and somehow thirty minutes passed in a blur."

Nothing wrong with her memory, clearly, and it was more than a little flattering that she recalled his clothing from that day.

"And there was something about me that you didn't like?" Obviously, or she wouldn't have matched him up with her sister. Maybe she'd only thought of him as a friend.

"Oh, no! You were great. Gorgeous and gentlemanly." The blush that never seemed far from the surface of her skin bloomed again, heightening the blue in her eyes. "I mean, I might have been a little starstruck, which is silly, considering how many celebrities I've done taxes for."

That pleased him even more than her pink-shirt comment, and he wanted to learn more about this selfless woman who'd apparently been a part of his life for a long time. "You're an accountant, then?"

"Not anymore. I gave up all my clients when… Vanessa died." She laughed self-consciously. "It's hard to retrain my brain to no longer say 'when Antonio and Vanessa died'."

The mention of his wife sent an unexpected

spike of sadness through his gut. "I don't remember being married to her. Did you think we'd be a good couple? Is that why you introduced us?"

All at once, a troubling sense of disloyalty effectively killed the discovery mode he'd fallen into with Caitlyn. He had no context for his relationship with Vanessa, but she'd been his wife and this woman was his sister-in-law. He shouldn't be thinking about Caitlyn as anything other than a temporary mother to his children. She'd probably be horrified at the direction of his thoughts.

"Oh. No, I mentioned that she was my sister and you asked to meet her. I don't think you even noticed me after that. Vanessa is—was—much more memorable than me."

"I beg to differ," he countered wryly, which pulled a smile out of her. "When I close my eyes, yours is the only face I can picture."

Apparently he couldn't help himself. Did he automatically flirt with beautiful women or just this one?

More blushing. But he wasn't going to apologize for the messed-up state of his mind or the distinct pleasure he'd discovered at baiting this delicate-skinned woman. He'd needed something that made him feel good. Was that so wrong?

"Well, she was beautiful and famous. I didn't blame you for wanting an introduction. Most people did."

"Famous?" Somehow that didn't seem like valid criteria for wishing to meet a woman.

Caitlyn explained that Vanessa starred on *Beacon Street*, a TV show beloved by millions of fans, and then with a misty sigh, Caitlyn waxed poetic about their fairy-tale wedding. "Vanessa wanted a baby more than anything. She said it was the only thing missing from your perfect marriage."

He'd heard everything she'd said, but in a removed way, as if it had happened to someone else. And perhaps in many respects, it had. He didn't remember being in love with Vanessa, but he'd obviously put great stock in her as a partner, lover and future mother of his children.

Part of his journey apparently lay in reconciling his relationship with the woman he'd married—so he could know if it was something he might want to do again, with another woman, at some point in the future. He needed to grieve his lost love as best he could and move on.

Perhaps Caitlyn had a role in this part of his recovery, as well. "I'd like to know more about Vanessa. Will you tell me? Or is it too hard?"

She nodded with a small smile. "It's hard. But it's good for me, too, to remember her. I miss her every day."

Launching into an impassioned tribute to her sister, Caitlyn talked with her hands, her animated face clearly displaying her love for Vanessa. But Antonio couldn't stop thinking about that moment against the wall, when he'd almost reached out to see what Caitlyn's glossy hair felt like. What might have happened between them all those years ago if he hadn't asked Caitlyn to introduce him to Vanessa?

It was madness to wonder. He would do well to focus on the present, where, thanks to Caitlyn, he'd forgotten about his headache. She'd begged him to allow her to stay under his roof and, frankly, it was easy to say yes because he needed her help. Incredible fortune had smiled on him since the plane crash, and he couldn't help feeling that Caitlyn was a large part of it.

Four

Instead of taking Antonio to the doctor, Caitlyn arranged for the doctor to come to the house the following afternoon. Antonio needed his space for as long as possible, at least until he got comfortable being in civilization again—or at least that was Caitlyn's opinion, and no one had to know that it fit her selfish desire to have him all to herself.

As a plus, Caitlyn wouldn't have to worry about wrestling Antonio into the car in case he changed his mind about seeing a doctor after all. Not that she could have. Nor did she do herself any favors imagining the tussle, which would likely end with Antonio's hard body pinning her against another wall.

Recalling yesterday's charged encounter had kept her quite warm last night and quite unable to sleep due to a restless ache she had no idea how to ease. Well, okay, she had *some* idea, but her sensibilities didn't extend to middle-of-the-night visits to the sexy man down the hall. One did not simply walk into Antonio's bedroom with the intent of hopping into bed with him, or at least *she* didn't. Risqué nighttime shenanigans were Vanessa's style, and her sister had had her heart broken time and time again as a result. Sex and love were so closely entwined that Caitlyn was willing to wait for the commitment she'd always wanted.

Nor did she imagine that Antonio was lying awake fantasizing about visiting Caitlyn anytime soon, either. They were two people thrown together by extraordinary circumstances and they both had enormous, daunting realities to deal with that didn't easily translate into any kind of relationship other than...what? Friends? Co-parents? Trying to figure it out was exhausting enough; adding romance to the mix was out of the question.

Especially since Antonio could—and likely would—have his pick of women soon enough. A virgin mother of triplets, former accountant sister-in-law didn't have the same appeal as a lush, redheaded actress-wife combo, that was for sure.

The doctor buzzed the gate entrance at precisely three o'clock. Antonio ushered the stately salt-and-pepper-haired physician into the foyer and thanked him for coming as the two men shook hands.

All morning, Antonio had been short-tempered and scowling, even after Caitlyn told him the doctor was coming to him. Caitlyn hovered just beyond the foyer, unsure if she was supposed to make herself scarce or insist on being present for the conversation in case the doctor had follow-up instructions for Antonio's care.

Vanessa would have been stuck to Antonio's side. As a wife should. Caitlyn was only the person who had made the appointment. And she'd done that just to make sure it happened.

"Caitlyn," Antonio called, his tone slightly

amused, which was a plus, considering his black mood. "Come meet Dr. Barnett."

That she could do. She stood by Antonio, but not too close, and exchanged pleasantries with the doctor.

"I saw you fight Alondro in Vegas," the doctor remarked with an appreciative nod at Antonio. "Ringside. Good match."

Antonio accepted the praise with an inclined head, but his hands immediately clenched and his mouth tightened; clearly, the doctor's comments made him uncomfortable. Because he didn't remember? Or had he lost all context of what it meant to be famous? Either way, she didn't like anyone making Antonio uncomfortable, let alone someone who was supposed to be here to help.

"Can I show you to a private room where you can get started?" Caitlyn asked in a no-nonsense way.

"Of course." Dr. Barnett's face smoothed out and he followed Caitlyn and Antonio to the master bedroom, where Antonio had indicated he felt the most at home in the house.

Score one for Caitlyn. Or was it two since a medical professional was on the premises?

She started to duck out, but Antonio stopped her with a warm hand on her arm. "I'd like you to stay," he murmured. "So it will feel less formal."

"Oh." A bit flummoxed, she stared up into his dark eyes. "It won't be weird if the doctor wants you to…um…get undressed?"

On cue, her cheeks heated. She'd blushed more around this man in the past few days than she had in her whole life.

His lips quirked and she congratulated herself on removing that dark scowl he'd worn all day. Too bad his new expression had come about because he likely found her naïveté amusing.

"It will only be weird if you make it weird." His head tilted as he contemplated her. "What kind of doctor's appointment do you think this is?"

She scowled in return. "I'll stay. But only if you stop making fun of me."

He winked. *Winked.* "I solemnly swear. Provided you stop saying things that are funny."

"And," she continued as if he hadn't tried to be charming and slick, when, in truth, it fluttered her heart to be so firmly in the sights of Antonio's weapons of choice. "I'll stay if you'll be perfectly honest with the doctor. If you aren't, I will be."

At that, he smiled. "Then, you'll definitely have to see me undressed."

"For what reason?" she hissed with a glance at the doctor, who was pretending not to listen to their far-too-loud discussion. Did Antonio have zero sense of propriety?

"Otherwise, how will you know what to say about my badly healed broken leg?" Antonio responded innocently and laughed as Caitlyn smacked his arm. Over his shoulder, he called, "Dr. Barnett, can we start out dressed or shall I strip immediately?"

Dr. Barnett cleared his throat. "We'll talk first and then I'll take some vital signs. A more…ah… thorough examination will only become necessary pending the outcome of our discussion. Ms. Hopewell is free to excuse herself at that point."

Even the doctor sounded as if Caitlyn's lack of experience around naked men was cause for hilarity. She firmed her mouth and sank into the chair Antonio indicated in the sitting area, which was thankfully far from the bed, then crossed her arms. *Men.*

And speaking of pigheaded males—why was she just *now* finding out Antonio had suffered a broken leg? It probably needed to be reset and it must pain him something awful and…it wasn't her business. She'd gotten him in front of a doctor; now someone with a medical degree could talk sense into the man, who apparently thought he'd turned immortal.

Dr. Barnett settled into a wing-back chair with a clipboard he'd pulled from his bag of tricks. After a quick back-and-forth with the patient to determine Antonio's age, approximate height and weight, the doctor took his heart rate and peered into his throat.

"Now, then." The doctor contemplated Antonio. "Ms. Hopewell indicated that you have trouble remembering your past. Can you tell me more about that?"

"No," Antonio said smoothly, but Caitlyn heard the obstinacy in his voice. "You're here because I have headaches. Make them go away."

Caitlyn frowned. *That* was the thing he was most worried about?

The doctor asked a few pointed questions about the nature of Antonio's pain, which he refused to answer. Dr. Barnett pursed his lips. "I can write you a prescription for some heavy-duty painkillers, but I'd like to do a CT scan first. I'm concerned about your purported memory loss coupled with headaches. I'd prefer to know what we're dealing with before treating the symptoms."

"No tests. Write the prescription," Antonio ordered and stood, clearly indicating the appointment was over whether the doctor wished it to be or not. "Ms. Hopewell misrepresented the nature of the medical care I need."

Caitlyn didn't move from her chair. "How long will the CT scan take? Will you get results immediately or will it only lead to more tests? Will you also look at his leg?"

Someone had to be the voice of reason here.

"It doesn't matter, because that's not the problem," Antonio cut in with a scowl. "I'm not sick. I'm not an invalid, and my leg is fine. I just need something to make my headaches manageable."

Dr. Barnett nodded. "Fine. I'll write you a prescription for a painkiller, but only for enough pills to get you through the next few days. If you go to the radiology lab and get the CT scan, I'll give you more."

"Blackmail?" Antonio's lips quirked, but no

one would mistake it for amusement. "I'll just find another doctor."

"Perhaps." Dr. Barnett shrugged. "Hollywood is certainly full of dishonest medical practitioners who will write prescriptions for just about anything if someone is willing to pay enough. Just keep in mind that many of those someones wind up in the morgue. I will never be a party to putting one of my patients there."

That was enough to convince Caitlyn she'd selected the right doctor, and she wasn't going to stand by and let Antonio destroy an opportunity to get the help he needed, not when he had three very good reasons to get better the medically approved way. "Dr. Barnett, please write the prescription for the amount of pills you think is appropriate and leave me the information about the radiology lab. We'll discuss it and get back to you."

Antonio crossed his arms, his expression the blackest it had been all day, but thankfully he kept his mouth closed instead of blasting her for interfering.

The doctor hastily scrawled on his pad and tore off the top page, handing it to Caitlyn with a business card for the radiology lab. She saw him out and shut the front door, assuming Antonio had stayed holed up in his room to work off his mood.

But when she turned, he was leaning against the wall at the other end of the foyer, watching her with crossed arms and a hooded, hard look. His expression wasn't as black as it had been, but somehow it was far more dangerous.

Startled, she backed up against the door, accidentally trapping her hands behind her. Feeling oddly exposed, she yanked them free and laced her fingers together over her abdomen, right where a strange sort of hum had started.

"I'm not getting a CT scan," he said succinctly. "I didn't ask you to call the doctor so you could railroad me into a bunch of useless tests. I had enough of doctors in Indonesia who couldn't fix me."

She shook her head, not about to back down. This was too important. "But what if the tests help? Don't you want to get your memory back?"

"Of course." A hint of vulnerability flitted through his gaze and the hum inside her abdomen sped up. "There's only one thing that's helped with that so far and it wasn't a doctor."

The atmosphere in the foyer pressed down on her, almost agonizing in its power. She couldn't think when he was like this, so focused and intense, funneling all of his energy toward her. It woke up her nerve endings and they ruffled under the surface of her skin, begging her to move with a restless insistence. But move where?

"What helps?" she asked softly, afraid of spooking him. She couldn't predict if he'd leave or advance on her and, at this point, she couldn't say which she'd prefer.

"Fighting." The word reverberated against the marble, ringing in her ears.

She gasped, hand flying to her mouth. Surely he didn't mean actual fighting. As if he intended to return to his former sport.

"I need to get in the ring again," he confirmed, his dark gaze on hers, searching for something she couldn't give him. Pleading with her to understand. "I have—"

"No," she interrupted as her stomach dropped. "You can't. You have no idea what's going on inside your skull and you want to introduce more trauma? Not a good idea."

He'd only returned to civilization a few days

ago, broken on the inside. He needed…something, yes, but it wasn't picking up his former MMA persona as if no time had passed. As if he was still whole and healthy. As if he had nothing important to lose.

"This is not your call, Caitlyn," he said gently. Too gently. He'd already made up his mind. "This is my life, my head. I'm a fighter. It's what I do."

She stared up at him, and the raw emotion swimming through his eyes took her breath. "You haven't been a fighter for a long time, Antonio. You're a businessman now."

That was the man she knew well, the safe, contained version of Antonio. When he'd quit his MMA career to manage what went on in the ring for other fighters, it was the best of both worlds. Antonio still had all the outer trappings of his lean fighting physique, which—*let's be honest*—was wickedly delicious enough to get a nun going, but he'd shed the harsh brutality of Falco.

She liked him as a businessman. Businessmen were constant, committed. The way she'd always thought of Antonio. If he wasn't that man, who was he?

"I might have been before the crash, but I don't

remember that part of me." Bleakly, he stared off into the distance and her heart plummeted. "That Antonio might as well be dead. The only Antonio *I* know is the one who lives inside my heart, beating against the walls of my chest, alive but not *whole*. That Antonio screams inside my head, begging to be free of this web of uncertainty."

God, how poetically awful and terrible. Her soul ached to imagine the confusion and pain he must experience every minute of every day, but at the same time, she thrilled in the knowledge that he'd shared even that small piece of himself.

His gaze snapped back to hers and she'd swear on a stack of Bibles he hadn't moved, but his heat wrapped around her, engulfing her, and she was powerless to stop it from affecting her. She wanted to step back, quickly. As fast as her legs could carry her. But he'd backed her against the wall...or she'd backed herself against the wall by starting this madness. By assuming she could convince a man who'd survived a plane crash to see a doctor.

Madness.

Because her body ached for Antonio to step into that scant space between them, which felt uncomfortably slight and yet as massive as the ocean that had separated him from his old life.

She wanted to support him. To care for him. To help him reenter his life in whatever way made sense to him. Who was she to say he shouldn't be in the ring again? Vanessa hadn't liked him fighting, either, but her sister had held many weapons in her arsenal that might have prevented the man she'd married from doing something dangerous.

Caitlyn had nothing.

"Please understand." He held her captive without words, without touching her at all, as his simple plea burned her throat. "I have to unleash my frustration on an opponent who can take it. Who's trained for it. Before I take it out on someone else."

Her teeth caught her lip and bit down as his meaning sank in. He sought a healthy outlet for his confusion, one that was familiar to him. Why was that so bad?

She'd been trying to keep him away from the media, away from his former employees and business partners, who might ask uncomfortable questions he couldn't answer. Perhaps she'd worried unnecessarily. Most likely, he'd be firmly in the public eye for the rest of his life, whether she liked it or not, and she couldn't keep him to herself forever. It was ridiculous to even pretend they could hide away in this house, even for a few days.

And then he reached out, encompassing her forearm with his palm. "I need you—" He swallowed and faltered. "I need you in my corner, Caitlyn. I don't have anyone else."

Wide-eyed, she covered his strong fingers with hers. Reassuringly, she squeezed, reveling in the contact as warmth flooded the places where their skin touched. *She* was comforting *him* in what was clearly a difficult conversation for them both.

He needed her. More important, he needed her to validate his choices, no matter how crazy they seemed.

A little awed by the realization, she nodded because speaking wasn't an option as he rested his forehead on hers, whispering his gratitude. She closed her eyes against the intimacy of the thank-you, feeling as if she'd just fought an exhausting battle, only to look up and see the opposing general's second flank swarming the battlefield.

"I'll take you to Falco," she promised, her voice

croaking, and wished she only meant she would take him to the building housing the empire he'd founded called Falco Fight Club. But she suspected she would really be taking him back to his former self, when he *was* Falco, a champion fighter who regularly took blows to the head.

God help her for enabling this lunacy.

Caitlyn insisted on driving to Falco, and Antonio humored her only because his pounding head had blurred his vision. Slightly. Not enough to give the doctor's ridiculous CT-scan idea any credence. He'd had plenty of brain scans in the past and the final one had ended his career.

He'd given up trying to understand why he could recall the last CT scan he'd endured, but couldn't remember the woman he'd been married to for—what? Four or five years? He didn't even know. He couldn't even fully picture her face, just bits of it in an insane collage.

They picked up Antonio's prescription on the way, but he waited to take a pill since the warning said the medication might make him drowsy. He definitely wanted to be alert for this first trip to his place of business.

The building came into view and Caitlyn pointed at it, saying Antonio had bought the lot and built Falco from the ground up, approving the architect's plans, surveying the drywall as it went up and hand selecting the equipment inside.

He waited for some sense of recognition. Pushed for it with widened eyes and a mostly empty mind. But the simple glass and brick looked like hundreds of other buildings in Los Angeles.

Falco Fight Club. The red-and-black letters marched across the brick, signifying this as the headquarters for the global MMA promotional company Antonio had founded. Under the name, a replica of the falcon tattoo on Antonio's pectoral had apparently been worked in as Falco's logo.

He briefly touched the ink under his shirt. This was part of his past, and likely his future as well, though he knew nothing about the business side of Falco. Nor did he have a driving desire to reclaim the helm...not yet.

He was here for what happened inside the ring.

Grimly, he climbed from the Range Rover Caitlyn drove more carefully than a ninety-year-old priest, and hesitated, suddenly fearful at crossing the threshold. What if he climbed into the ring and none of his memories came back? What if Caitlyn was right and additional trauma to his head actually caused more problems? He was a father now; he had other people to think about besides himself.

Caitlyn's presence wrapped around him before she slipped her smooth hand into his. It felt oddly...right to have her by his side as he faced down his past. She didn't say a word but stood with him as he surveyed the entrance, silently offering her unconditional support, even though she'd been adamantly against him fighting.

Somehow, that made his unsettling confusion acceptable. No matter what happened inside Falco Fight Club, he'd found his old life, and after a year of praying for it, he'd count his blessings.

The falcon emblem on his chest mirrored the one on the bricks in more ways than one—both decorated a shell housing the soul of Antonio Cavallari, and somewhere inside lay the answers he sought. He wouldn't give up until he had reclaimed *all* of his pieces.

"Is the company still in operation?" he asked, wishing he'd unbent from his bad mood enough to ask the question in the car. But his headache had grown worse as the day wore on, and he was weary of dealing with pain and questions and the blankness inside his head.

She nodded. "I get monthly reports from the interim CEO, Thomas Warren. He's been running it in your stead, but I have no idea if he's doing a good job or not. I was hoping you'd want to take over at some point, but I think everyone would understand if you didn't do so right away."

"Do they know?" He inclined his head toward the building, and even that renewed the pounding at his temples. Maybe he should take a painkiller anyway. It might dull the embarrassment and frustration of not knowing who "they" were.

She squeezed his hand and let it go, then shoved hers into her pocket. He missed the feel of her skin on his instantly and almost reached for her but recognized the wisdom in not appearing too intimate in public.

"Thomas called me yesterday after your lawyer gave him the heads-up that you were back," she said. "But I didn't tell him anything other than to confirm it was true, which was all he asked. I didn't know how much you'd planned to divulge."

"Thanks." He didn't know, either, but the truth

would likely come out soon enough when Antonio stepped inside and had to be led around his own building like a blind person.

"Antonio." She hesitated for a moment. "I've been trying to shield you from the media, but you should know that coming to Falco is probably going to trip their radar. You should be prepared for a full onslaught at any time."

A crush of people, cameras, microphones, babbling. The chants of "Falco, Falco, Falco." The montage was the clearest yet of elements from his past. The memory washed over him, or rather it was a blend of several memories bleeding together, of him leaving the ring to follow his manager as Rick pushed through the crowd.

With the images came the expected renewed headache. The increased pounding and pressure wasn't so difficult to deal with if it came with new memories. But it was a brutal trade-off.

"I…" He'd been about to say he was used to reporters and cameras. But then he realized. The media wouldn't be interviewing him about his latest bout with Ramirez or Fuentes. He wasn't a fighter anymore.

Instead, the media would ask him painful questions, like, "Why don't you remember your wife?" and "What did you do for a whole year while you were gone?"

They might even ask him something even more difficult to answer, like, "How does it feel to find out you're a father after all this time?" Would the media want to crack open his life and take pictures of his children? He didn't want the babies exposed to anyone who didn't necessarily have their best interests at heart.

Caitlyn had been *shielding* him from the media. As if she wanted to protect him. It snagged a tender place inside, and he had no idea what to do with that.

"I shouldn't have come here," he muttered and turned to climb back into the Range Rover.

Fight or flight. The more he delved into his past, the more appropriate the name Falco became. Seemed as if Antonio was constantly poised to use his talons or his wings, and he didn't like it. But he had no idea how to change it, how to achieve a happy medium where he dealt with life in a healthy way.

"Wait."

Caitlyn stopped him with a warm hand on his

shoulder and the area under her palm tingled. Did all women affect him so greatly, or just this one?

Aggravated because he couldn't remember, Antonio moved out of her reach but paused before sliding into the passenger seat.

"I wasn't trying to talk you out of going inside," she said, concern lacing her tone. Enough so that he turned to face her. "This is important to you, and I think you need to do it. Five minutes. We'll walk around, say hello and then leave. The press won't have time to congregate in that length of time if you'd prefer not to be accosted."

"And then what?" he asked far more sharply than he'd intended, but she didn't flinch. "The hurdles will still be there tomorrow and the next day."

And he didn't just mean the press. All at once, the uphill battle he faced to reclaim his memories, coupled with the constant physical pain, overwhelmed him.

"That will be true whether you take this step or not." She held out her hand for him to clasp, as if she'd known exactly what he needed.

Without hesitation, he slid his hand into hers

and held it, wordlessly absorbing her energy and spirit, and it calmed him instantly. Miraculously.

"Walk with me." She pulled him away from the car and shut the door. "I'll do all the talking. If you want to spar with someone, the training facility is adjacent to the administrative offices. I'm sure one of the guys would indulge you in a round. There's always a ton of people either in the rings or strength training on the gym equipment."

"How do you know so much about my company?" he asked as he let her lead him toward the door, his pulse hammering in his temples. From nerves, trauma, the silky-sweet scent of Caitlyn? He couldn't tell. Maybe it was all three.

"I spent time here occasionally over the past year." A shadow passed through her expression. "I've brought the babies a couple of times, hoping to infuse your heritage into them. Silly, I know. They're too young to understand it."

She laughed and he felt an answering tug at his mouth. How did she do that? He'd been all set to command her to drive away as fast as she could, and when he got home, he'd probably have barred himself in his room to indulge in a fit of bad temper. Instead, Caitlyn had gotten him across the parking lot and pulled a smile from him, as well.

All in the name of physically, mentally and spiritually guiding him through a place she hadn't wanted him to go.

What an amazing, beautiful, selfless woman. The mother of his children. There was nothing temporary about her role; he saw that now. Her love for them shone through in every action, every small gesture.

Caitlyn Hopewell was his children's mother, and it was an odd addition to her attractiveness. But there it was.

That ever-present sense of disloyalty squelched the warmth in his chest that had bloomed at the sound of Caitlyn's laugh. Caitlyn was sensual and beautiful and likely that meant her sister'd had those qualities, as well. But why couldn't he remember being so outrageously attracted to Vanessa? Why couldn't he remember her touch the way he could recall with perfect clarity what Caitlyn's hand felt like on his shoulder? Surely he'd fallen for Vanessa for a myriad of reasons, especially if he'd married the redheaded sister instead of the dark-haired one. His late wife's attributes and personality must have eclipsed Caitlyn's.

But he couldn't fathom how, not when innocently thinking about Caitlyn caused a burn in his gut he couldn't explain away. It was pure, sensual attraction that he wished to explore.

How was he supposed to move past his relationship with Vanessa and potentially have a new one—especially if the woman was Caitlyn—when thinking about moving on caused a wretched sense of unfaithfulness?

Five

Antonio stepped through the glass doors to Falco with a silent sense of awe. The reception area held a hushed purpose, as if to say important matters happened between these walls, and it hit him oddly to imagine he owned all of this, had made it happen, had created this company himself through his own ingenuity and resolve.

White marble stretched under his feet, edged with red and black. Framed promotional pictures lined the walls on both sides, similar to the ones in his home gym, featuring fierce-faced fighters with raised gloves or crossed arms sporting bulging biceps. Many wore enormous title belts with distinctive, rounded shields in the center, proclaiming the fighter a world champion.

His own face stared back at him from three of the frames, one each for his three welterweight titles. The memory of posing for the shots crowded into his head, crystal clear.

But he couldn't remember picking out the marble under his feet or the lot under the foundation or ever having walked into this building before today. It was becoming evident that his most severe memory loss encompassed the events that had happened after that final knockout Caitlyn had spoken of, the one that had ended his fighting career.

Perhaps the CT scan wasn't such a far-fetched next step. If there was something in his brain locking up his memories of that period, shouldn't he explore options to remove the block? Of course, he barely remembered Vanessa and he didn't remember Caitlyn at all, though he'd clearly known them both prior to his career-ending coma. So nothing was guaranteed.

After all, none of the Indonesian doctors had helped. Nothing had helped. And he hated hoping for a cure that would eventually amount to nothing.

In deference to the holidays, the reception area held a small decorated tree, and holly boughs covered nearly every surface. A classic Bing Crosby tune filtered through the sound system and he recognized it, of course, because his brain retaining Christmas songs made perfect sense. The receptionist looked up from her desk, blonde and perky, smiling with genuine happiness when she saw Antonio.

"Mr. Cavallari!" She shook her head, her wide-eyed gaze searching his face. "It's as if the past year never happened. I can't believe it. You look exactly the same."

Antonio nodded, because what else would he do when he couldn't remember this woman's name, though he'd probably hired her.

"Hi, Mandy," Caitlyn said smoothly, as if she'd read his mind. "Antonio would like to see what you've done with the place in his absence. I assured him that Thomas and his stellar team kept things in order, but there's nothing like an in-person tour, right?"

Rescued again. Antonio squelched the gratefulness flooding his chest, because how long could Caitlyn's savior superpowers actually last? It was a fluke anyway. There was no way she'd picked up on his distress. They barely knew each other and besides, her ability to read his mind had to be flawed; *he* didn't even know what was in his head most of the time.

"Of course." The receptionist—Mandy—smiled at Caitlyn and picked up the phone on the desk to murmur into it, then glanced up again. "Thomas will be here momentarily to show you around. Glad you're…um…*here*, Mr. Cavallari."

Here, meaning not dead. That was definitely a plus and cheered him slightly. "Thanks, Mandy. I plan to be around for a long time."

A man with a graying crew cut wearing an expensive, tailored suit bustled into the reception area. *Thomas.*

A memory of the two of them standing in nearly this same spot popped into Antonio's head, from Thomas's first day on the job. Relief stung the back of Antonio's throat. His memories were in there somewhere. It just took the right combination of criteria for them to battle to the forefront.

Thomas Warren was flanked by a couple of younger men in sweatpants and hoodies. Fighters. They wore almost identical expressions with a slight menacing edge, and they both leaned into the room, fists lightly curled as if preparing to start swinging.

Antonio recognized the stance instantly—he'd entered thousands of rooms that way. Still did, even now. Or perhaps he'd only picked it up again recently. Had he lost that ready-to-fly edge in the past few years, only to regain it after awakening to a blank world where simply entering a room brought on a barrage of questions and few answers?

These were the pieces of Antonio Cavallari he hoped to recover inside this building.

"Thomas." Antonio held out his hand to the older man, who shook Antonio's hand with a critical once-over.

"It's true." The interim CEO of Falco Fight Club narrowed his gaze, mouth slightly open as he fixated on Antonio's face. "I guess you can call me a doubting Thomas because I really didn't believe it until I saw you for myself. Come, let me show you the improvements we've made in your…ah, absence."

Seemed as if everyone was going to stumble over the proper verbiage to explain they'd assumed Antonio had died in the plane crash. He didn't blame them; he didn't have any clue what you were supposed to say, either.

"Let's put pretense aside," Antonio said before he'd fully determined what he planned to say. "You thought I was dead and spent the past year accordingly. I may disagree with some, or even all, of your decisions, but I fail to see how I could find fault with them. You did what you thought was right and I have no intention of walking in here to undo everything you've done."

Thomas's eyebrows rose. "Fair enough. It is an unprecedented situation and I appreciate that we might both need to maintain flexibility."

Thomas inclined his head and indicated Antonio should follow him into the interior of the building.

The two fighters fell in behind as well, and Antonio had the distinct sense the men were either intended as intimidation or accessory. It didn't matter which; either one was as laughable as it was baffling.

The short tour generated little in the way of jogging his memories, but the visit to Falco itself had already yielded a valuable harvest. Antonio had the unique opportunity to appreciate what he'd built using his own fortitude and business savvy as he surveyed it for what was, for all intents and purposes, the first time.

The vast influence of Falco unrolled before him as he learned of his vision for bringing glory back to the sport of mixed martial arts with a promotional powerhouse that had no ties to a media conglomerate. Untainted by corporate politics or the need for a healthy bottom line, Antonio had pushed boundaries, opening MMA to unconventional fighting disciplines, training some of the most elite fighters in the world and gaining entry to off-the-beaten-path venues. Most important, he'd insisted all his fighters be allowed to compete for titles based on their records, not handshake promotional deals.

And he'd been wildly successful, beyond anything he'd envisioned when Caitlyn mentioned Falco was where he'd made all his money. When he'd asked Thomas to show him the books, his eye had shot straight to the profit line, as if he'd last glanced at a balance sheet yesterday. The number of decimal places couldn't be right, and Antonio had nearly chalked it up to a clerical error until he glanced at the rest of the line items.

Not a mistake. Billions of dollars flowed through his company. It was dizzying. He should have paid more attention to the balances of his accounts when Caitlyn had transferred control of his estate back to him at his lawyer's office the other day.

No wonder Caitlyn hadn't taken the first opportunity to get out of Dodge when he'd offered to relieve her of baby duty. He could easily give her eight or nine figures for her trouble and never think twice about it, which was probably what she was hoping for. She seemed to genuinely care about the children, but everyone wanted something, and that something tended to be money.

"I want to see the training facility," Antonio announced abruptly.

"Absolutely." Thomas led the way to the adjacent building.

Energy bolted through his body as he anticipated climbing between the ropes. That had been his sole purpose in coming here and it had thus far been eclipsed by a slow slide back into Businessman Antonio.

Which didn't seem as bad as it once might have.

Maybe part of his journey lay in coupling both halves of his soul—the fighter and the suit—under one banner. But it wouldn't be today. He needed to get his wits about him, what few remained, and the ring was the only place where he'd experienced any peace in the past year.

As he entered the training facility, Antonio's lungs hitched as his eye was drawn to the equipment closet, to the three rings, one with a regulation metal cage surrounding it, to the workout area. Exactly where he'd known they would all be placed. Because he truly remembered, or because he'd modeled the layout on another facility from before the career-ending knockout?

Eager to find out, he strode through the cavernous room, drawing the attention of the muscled men—and surprisingly, a few women—engaged in various activities. One by one, weights drifted to the ground and sparring partners halted, gloves down, as they stared at him.

"That's right," he called to the room at large. "I've arisen from my watery grave. Who's brave enough to go a round with a ghost?"

"Cavallari, you sly dog." A grinning Hispanic male, early twenties, jogged over from his spot at a weight bench and punched Antonio on the arm as if he'd done it often. "They told us you were dead. What have you been doing, hiding out to get back in professional shape without any pressure? Smart."

What a ridiculous notion. Ridiculously brilliant. Maybe he'd adopt it as his easy out if the media did start harassing him about his whereabouts over the past year.

"Hey, Rodrigo," Caitlyn called, and when Antonio glanced at her, she winked, and then murmured under her breath, "Rodrigo was a good friend. Before."

When they got home, he'd treat her to the most expensive bottle of wine in his cellar. And then when she was good and looped, he'd carefully extract her real agenda.

No matter how much she seemed to love his kids, no one did nice things without a motive. He wanted to know what hers was.

"Are you my volunteer?" Antonio jerked his head at the nearest ring, eyes on his potential sparring partner.

"Sure, boss." Rodrigo shadowboxed a couple of jabs at Antonio's gut. "Like old times. Just go easy on me if your secret training put you out of my league."

Rodrigo's grin belied the seriousness of the statement—did he not believe Antonio had actually trained over the past year or did he assume that regardless, they'd still be matched in skill? Apparently, they'd sparred before and had been on pretty equal ground.

"Likewise," Antonio commented, mirroring Rodrigo's grin because it felt expected. Honestly, he had no idea how they'd match up. He couldn't wait to find out.

Something inside rotated into place, as if two gears had been grinding together haphazardly, and all at once, the teeth aligned, humming like a well-oiled machine.

His headache had almost receded and if God had been listening to his pleas at all, the next few minutes would knock loose a precious memory or two.

* * *

Before long, Antonio had slipped into the shorts Caitlyn had insisted he bring from home. She watched him face off against Rodrigo in the large ring, both men bare-chested and barefoot. It hadn't taken the office grapevine but about five minutes to circulate the news that Antonio Cavallari was both back and in the ring. Nearly everyone from FFC's administrative building had crowded into the training facility and around the cage with expectant faces, murmuring about Antonio's return.

You couldn't have pried most of the women's gazes from Antonio with a crowbar, Caitlyn's included, though she at least tried to hide it. But he was magnificent, sinewy and hard, with that fierce tattoo so prominent against his golden body. His still-longish hair was slicked back from his forehead, highlighting his striking eyes as they glittered like black diamonds.

Apparently she liked him as a fighter just as much as she liked the savvy businessman. Maybe more. Her raw reaction at the sight of Antonio in the ring was powerful and uncomfortably warm.

Hot, even. And far lower than seemed appropriate in public.

It was shameful. Shameful to be so affected by her sister's husband, shameful that she'd carried a yet-to-be-extinguished torch for Antonio all of these years. Most shameful of all was that at least half of his appeal lay in his primal stance as he waited for an opening to do bodily harm to another human. She'd always thought of him as the perfect man—committed, beautiful, steady. And it frightened her to be so attracted to him for purely carnal reasons.

But she couldn't stop the flood of elemental longing any more than she could explain how over-the-top sexy the man had become once he slipped into his glory in the ring.

She'd never seen him fight live. Once he and Vanessa had hooked up, she'd spent a lot of time feeling sorry for herself and as little time as possible around the two of them. It was too hard to be reminded that he'd picked the glamorous Hopewell sister instead of the quiet, unassuming one. Not that she blamed him; most men had overlooked Caitlyn in favor of Vanessa, and Caitlyn had never been bitter about it. Until Antonio.

She'd spent the entirety of their marriage hiding her hurt and disappointment and jealousy, the entirety of their relationship wishing she could have her sister's marriage…and then the past year feeling guilty and sick about the uncharitable thoughts she'd had.

Now she just wanted to feel as if she didn't have to apologize for being alive when her sister wasn't. For being a woman affected by a prime specimen of man as he engaged in physical combat. Was that so wrong?

The men circled each other, trash-talking. Suddenly, Antonio lashed out in a blur of intricately executed moves, both beautiful and lethally graceful. Her breath caught as she drank in the visual panorama. Antonio's body moved fluidly, as if it had been made specifically for this purpose, and it was stunning to behold.

In enabling him to return to the ring, she'd unwittingly exposed herself to a piece of his soul that was the opposite of harsh, the opposite of brutal. It was breathtaking.

Caitlyn blinked as Rodrigo hit the mat without having lodged one defense.

Violence was unfolding before her very eyes

and the only thing she'd noticed was how exquisitely Antonio had executed it. Something was very wrong with her.

The crowd murmured as Rodrigo shook his head and climbed to his feet, rubbing his jaw.

"Lucky shot, boss," he grumbled.

Not that she had any basis for judgment, but Caitlyn didn't think so. As the men went at it again, Antonio's superior skill and style couldn't be mistaken, even by an untrained eye such as hers. Rodrigo landed a couple of shots, but the younger man called a halt to the match after only a few more minutes, breathing heavily. Caitlyn grimaced at his split lip.

Rodrigo and Antonio shook hands and the crowd slowly dispersed, many of them stopping to welcome Antonio back or clap him on the shoulder with a few congratulatory words about his performance.

Caitlyn hung back, remaining as unobtrusive as possible while Antonio excused himself to shower and change. No one was paying attention to her anyway, which she considered a blessing as long as her insides were still so unsettled. This whole Falco Fight Club experience had shown her something about herself that she didn't understand and didn't know what to do with.

Antonio returned. His gaze cut through the crowd and locked on to hers, his eyes dark with something untamed and unnameable and she shivered. It was as if he knew exactly where she was in the crowd. And exactly what she'd been thinking about while watching him fight.

Her cheeks heated and she blessed his distance because, hopefully, that meant he couldn't tell. But the distance disappeared as he strode directly to her.

Though clothed, his potency hadn't diminished in the slightest. Because she knew what his hard body looked like under his crisp white shirt and slacks. Heat rolled between them and his gaze fell to her mouth for a moment as if he was thinking about dropping a kiss there.

Her lips tingled under his scrutiny. Madness. She'd fallen under some kind of spell that caused her imagination to run away with her, obviously.

"I'm ready to go home," he murmured and the moment broke apart. "I've had enough for one day."

"Sure," she managed to get out around the tight, hot lump in her throat.

Goody. Now they could cram themselves into a tiny Range Rover for the drive home, where his masculine scent would overpower her, and she'd spend the drive reminding herself that no matter how sexy he was, the complications between them were legion.

Which was exactly what happened. She gripped the wheel, white-knuckling it onto the main street and, thankfully, Antonio fell silent.

Too silent. He'd just reentered his old world in the most immersive way possible. She desperately wanted to ask him about it.

Had he remembered any of Falco? All of it? What had it felt like for him to get in the ring again? Antonio hadn't fought professionally in years and, as far as Caitlyn knew, Vanessa had forbid him from even messing around with the guys in the ring because she feared he'd get hurt again.

Part of Caitlyn wondered if she'd helped facilitate his return to Falco because it was something her sister never would have done. As if it was some kind of sick contest to see if Antonio would realize Caitlyn was the better woman for him.

But she had no idea how to navigate the heavy vibe in the Range Rover, so she kept her mouth shut and let the silence ride.

When they got home, she followed him into the house from the garage, unable to stand the silence any longer. "How's your head?"

That was a safe enough topic, wasn't it?

He paused in the kitchen to get a glass of water and gulped the entire thing down before answering. "It hurts."

She leaned a hip on the granite countertop as close to him as she dared and crossed her arms over her still-unsettled insides. "Why don't you take a painkiller and rest."

"Because I'm not ninety and waiting around to die," he said shortly, then frowned. "Sorry, I don't mean to snap."

The line between his eyebrows concerned her and she regretted not encouraging him to talk to her while they'd been in the car. Her own uncertainties weren't an excuse to be selfish. "It's okay. You've had a difficult day."

His gaze latched on to hers and he surveyed

her with a focused, hooded expression that pulled at something deep in her core. In or out of the ring—didn't matter. He exuded a primal energy that she couldn't stop herself from reacting to, and it was as frightening as it was thrilling.

The way Antonio made her feel had nothing to do with the safe, nebulous fantasy she'd carried around in her heart for years. *That*, she understood. The raw, ferocious draw between them, she didn't.

"Difficult?" he repeated. "Really? What gives you that impression?"

"Uh…because you're snapping at me?" When the corners of his mouth lifted, she smiled involuntarily in return. "It couldn't have been easy to get into the ring today in front of all your colleagues. How long has it been since you last went a round?"

"A couple of weeks. I trained six hours a day in Indonesia over the past few months. It was part of my rehabilitation."

"Oh, you never mentioned that." And why would he? She wasn't his confidante. But she'd kind of hoped he saw her in that role, as someone he could turn to, who would be there for him in a confusing world.

"It wasn't worth mentioning." A smile still played with his lips and she couldn't tear her gaze from his mouth as he talked. "Indonesia was about survival. Only. I fight—then and now—because I have to."

The confessions of his deepest self were as affecting as watching him fight had been. She wanted more but was afraid of what it might mean to get it. "I remember you said you needed to get in the ring to blow off frustration. Did it work?"

"Partially," he allowed. "I need a more skilled partner."

"Yes, even I could see that Rodrigo was outmatched."

A blanket of intimacy settled around them as a full, genuine smile bloomed on his face, and she reveled in it.

Brigitte bustled into the kitchen at that moment, shattering the mood. "Oh, you're back. Grand. Do you want to spend time with the babies before dinner?"

Taking a guilty step backward, Caitlyn tore her

gaze from Antonio to focus on the au pair. "Um, yes. Of course."

She always played with the babies before dinner while Brigitte helped the chef, Francesco, put the children's meal together. What was wrong with Caitlyn that she hadn't noticed the time? Well, duh—Antonio was what was wrong with her.

"They're in their cribs waiting for you," Brigitte said sunnily and went to the fridge to pull out covered bowls of premashed fruit and veggies.

"Come with me." Caitlyn put a hand on Antonio's arm before she thought better of it. Heat prickled her palm and she snatched it back. "It'll be fun. Low pressure."

Fun, plus an excuse to stay in his presence under the pretense of guiding his steps toward fatherhood—but with the added distance the babies would automatically create.

Then she remembered his headache. "You don't have to if you'd rather be alone. I don't want to push you into a role you're not ready for."

"I'd like to," he said, surprising her.

He followed her upstairs and into the nursery. Leon stood in the center of his crib, both chubby hands gripping the edge to support his wobbly legs as he yowled like a wet cat. Annabelle sat with her back to the room banging one of the crib slats with a rattle while sweet Antonio Junior lay on his back staring at the mobile above his crib.

"There you go," Caitlyn murmured to their father. "This is a perfect encapsulation of your children's personalities. Leon does not like being forced to do something and he isn't a bit hesitant to tell you how unhappy he is. He'll be the first to learn how to climb out of his crib, mark my words. God help us then."

"Why?" Antonio eyed first his son and then Caitlyn as she boosted Leon from his crib and into her arms, which predictably, quieted down his protests.

"Because then he'll be a holy terror, climbing out in the middle of the night while we're asleep." She nodded to the baby. "Would you like to hold him?"

"Yes," he said decisively and then his brows drew together as Caitlyn handed over the baby. "Do I have to do anything?"

"Nothing special, just make sure he feels secure."

She laughed as Leon peered up at his father

suspiciously, as if trying to figure out whether he was okay with this new person. They'd learn the verdict in about two seconds.

Thankfully, Leon waved his fist around, which was his way of saying things were cool. Antonio's gaze never left his son's face, and his clear adoration shot straight through Caitlyn's heart with a painful, wonderful arrow.

Caitlyn spun to busy herself with Antonio Junior before the tears pricking at her eyelids actually fell in a mortifying display of sentiment. It was just a dad with his kid. Why should it be so tender and meaningful?

There were so many reasons locked up in that question, she could hardly start answering it—but first and foremost, because it was her kid, too, one she'd created with this man in a most unconventional way, sure, but that didn't make it any less powerful to watch the two interact.

Then there was the compelling contrast between this tender version of Antonio and the fierce warrior he'd been in the ring. The dichotomy created an even more compelling man, and he was already so mesmerizing, she could hardly think.

Antonio Junior hadn't made a sound since

they'd entered the room, so Caitlyn checked on him as she often did, just to be sure he was still breathing. He'd always been quiet, carrying the weight of the world on his shoulders, and it bothered her that he'd adopted such a grave demeanor.

He definitely took after his father in that respect, where Leon was a demanding prima donna like Vanessa.

"That's my serious little man," she crooned to Antonio Junior and slid her fingertips across his fine dark hair as he refocused his gaze from the mobile to Caitlyn.

The sheer beauty of her child nearly took her breath. She'd always thought he looked like Antonio, but it had been an academic observation based on memory and expectation—they both had dark hair and dark eyes; of course the comparisons would come.

"Is he serious?" Antonio asked with genuine curiosity.

"Very. He's also quiet. Annabelle would probably be content to sit in her crib until the cows came home as long as she could make noise," Caitlyn called over her shoulder and, dang it, her voice caught on the emotion still clogging her throat. She cleared it, hoping Antonio had been too caught up in Leon to notice. "That's her favorite thing. Noise. She likes it best when she can bang on something and then imitate the noise with her voice and, trust me, she practices a lot."

"I don't mind," Antonio said softly, and she sensed him come up behind her long before she heard his quiet intake of breath. He peered over her shoulder into Annabelle's crib. "Hi, there, sweetheart."

Annabelle tipped her head up to focus on her father, her upside-down face beaming. "Gah."

"Is that her imitation of banging the rattle?" Antonio asked with a laugh. "Because she should practice some more."

"No, that's how she says hello."

Caitlyn's throat tightened again, which was silly when she was only explaining her children's quirks. But their father didn't know any of these things—because he'd been lost and alone half a world away while she'd lived in his house, cared for his children and spent his money. She wanted to make that up to him as best she could.

"Come on, you big flirt." Caitlyn hoisted Annabelle out of the crib and set her on the soft pink blanket already spread out on the nursery floor. "I realize pink is clichéd for a girl, but I thought Annabelle needed girlie things with two brothers."

"You don't have to justify your choices." Antonio crouched down on the blanket and settled Leon next to his sister. "I'd be the last person to tell you you're doing it wrong, and even if I have a conflicting opinion, I'd prefer to talk through it, not issue countercommands. You've done the best you can, and it couldn't have been easy to do it alone."

"It wasn't." One tear spilled over before she could catch it. "I worried every day that I wasn't enough for them."

Antonio glanced up from his perch on the fluffy pink blanket, which should have looked ridiculous but didn't in the slightest. "You've been amazing. More than enough. Look at how perfect these babies are. Healthy, happy. What more could you have provided?"

"A father," she whispered. And somehow the fates had granted that wish in the most unexpected, flawless way possible. "They deserve two parents."

A shadow passed over his face. "And for now, that's what they have."

For now? Was that a cryptic comment about the future of her place in this family?

"No matter what happens, I will always be their mother," she stated firmly, and if only her voice hadn't cracked, it might have sounded as authoritative out loud as it had in her head.

They needed to talk about the future, but she was afraid to bring it up, afraid to overload him with one more thing he didn't want to deal with, afraid he was only letting her stay because it was Christmas and she'd begged him not to kick her out.

But she had to get over it and go to the mat for her children. If anyone could understand the bone-deep need to fight for what you wanted, it would surely be Antonio.

"Yes," he said quietly. "You *are* their mother."

And that took the wind out of her sails so fast, she couldn't breathe. "Okay, then."

She'd have to bring up the future another time, after she'd recovered from all of this.

Six

Antonio's headache persisted through dinner, but he couldn't stomach the idea of taking the pills now that he actually had them. He'd lost so much of his past; losing his present to drowsiness held little appeal. Instead, he bided his time until Caitlyn and Brigitte put the babies to bed and then he cornered Caitlyn in the sunroom.

He hoped she wouldn't mind the interruption. It was time to dig into what Caitlyn wanted from him in exchange for the role she'd played thus far in his life and the lives of his children. And did she see a continued role? If so, what role did she envision for herself?

The sun had set long ago and Caitlyn read by

low lamplight. He started to say her name but the words dried up on his tongue. Something inside lurched sweetly, as confusing as it was intriguing. Silently, he watched her, loath to alert her to his presence until he was good and finished sating himself on her ethereal beauty.

But she glanced up almost instantly, as if she'd sensed him. He knew the feeling. There was an undeniable draw between them, and he'd bet every last dollar that she felt it, too. Maybe it was time to dig into that as well, and find out what role *he* wanted her to play.

"Have a glass with me?" He held up the uncorked bottle of wine he'd judiciously selected from his extensive wine cellar.

"Um, sure." Her fair skin bloomed with that blush he liked far more than he should. But what had brought it out? He had a perverse need to find out.

Which seemed to be the theme of this nighttime rendezvous. He'd barely scratched the surface of what made Caitlyn Hopewell tick, and exposing her layers appealed to him immensely.

Antonio poured two glasses of the deep red cabernet and handed one to Caitlyn, then settled into the other chair, separated from hers by a small wooden end table. For a moment, he watched the moonlight dance on the silvery surf so beautifully framed by the wall of glass opposite the chairs.

"I bought this house specifically for the view from this room," he commented instead of diving right in. "It's my favorite spot."

"Mine, too," Caitlyn agreed quietly.

"I figured. This is where I find you most often." He sipped his wine, rolling it around on his tongue as the easy silence stretched. For once, Caitlyn didn't seem determined to fill the gap with nervous chatter.

It was nice to sit with no expectations and not worry about his missing memories. His headache eased the longer he watched the waves crash on the shore below.

"Did you have something on your mind?" she blurted out and then sighed. "I mean, other than the regular stuff, like becoming a father and having amnesia and learning to live in civilization again and—"

"Caitlyn." He touched the rim of his glass to hers in silent apology for the interruption, but he wasn't really sorry. He liked that she gave him so many opportunities to say her name. "I wanted to have a bottle of wine with you. As you pointed out, if nothing else, we're a family by default. Nothing wrong with acting like one."

She didn't relax. "Except we're not a family, not really. You were all set to send me on my way until I convinced you to let me stay through the holidays. Then what, Antonio? I need to know what you plan to do."

Nothing like laying it on the line. Apparently, the easy silence hadn't been so easy for her. If she wasn't keen on a social drink, they didn't have to play nice. Shame. He'd have preferred to have the wine flowing before getting to the reason he'd tracked her down.

But clearly, her ability to read him wasn't a fluke, as he'd assumed earlier today.

"I'm not sure," he said carefully. "It's not January yet and I have a lot to consider. Tell me what you'd like to see happen."

Her fingers gripped the stem of the wineglass until her nail beds turned white. "That's difficult to answer."

Because she didn't want to come right out and say that on the first of January, she'd take a wire transfer with nine zeros tacked onto the end? "Then, maybe you can answer this for me. Why did you rescue me at Falco so many times today? It was as if you could read the room and tell exactly when I was floundering."

"Oh, um..." Her eyebrows drew together as her gaze flew to his face, searching it, and unexpected rawness sprang into the depths of her eyes. "I don't know. It was painfully obvious when you didn't remember someone. I hated that you were uncertain."

That rawness—it nearly eviscerated him with its strength. What did it mean? He had no context for it, not with her, not with any woman. And he wanted to know if it signified the same intense desire to explore each other, the way it did in him.

The draw between them grew tighter as he contemplated her. "Obvious?"

"Well, probably not to everyone," she corrected quickly. "To me anyway. I was, uh...paying attention."

Her gaze traveled down his body, and she didn't try to hide it, probably because she had no idea how to play coy. Heat flared in his loins as he became extremely aware of how the lamp highlighted the curves under her clothes. "I never thanked you for paying such close *attention*. I'm curious, though. What do you hope to gain from helping me?"

"Gain?" She cocked her head, confusion evident. "I'm helping you navigate your life because you need me. You told me so. I want to help."

"Why?"

"Because I like the fact that you need me!" Her eyelids flew shut and she shook her head. Leaping to her feet, she backed away. "I didn't mean to say that."

"Caitlyn." He'd upset her, and he didn't like the way it snagged at his gut to be responsible for the distress around her mouth and eyes.

He'd much rather be responsible for the raw intensity he'd glimpsed a moment ago.

When he slid from his chair and approached her, she stood her ground despite the fact that her body was poised to flee.

"Wait," he murmured. "What did you mean to say?"

She wouldn't meet his gaze. "I meant to say that the children are my first priority."

No, there was more here, more she didn't want

to say, more she didn't want him to discover—
and that unidentified something called to him.

Instinct alone guided his hand to her chin and
he tipped her head up to evaluate her stricken
expression. "Mine, too. That's why I ask these
questions. I want to know whether you're helping me in hopes of a nice payout. Or some other,
yet-to-be-determined motive."

"Really, Antonio?" Fire flared in her blue eyes,
surprising him in its intensity. "Do you have any
context for what being a mother means? What it
means to me personally?"

Her lips curled into a harsh smile and he
couldn't stop watching her, fascinated by the
physical changes in her as she schooled him. Even
more surprising, she didn't pull away but pushed
her chin deeper into his grip.

"Leon, Annabelle and Antonio Junior are my
children," she continued, her voice dipping lower
with each impassioned word. "Just as much as
they're yours. More so. I carried them in my
womb and I've raised them. I could do it on an
accountant's salary and would have if the judge
hadn't granted me conservatorship of their inheritance. Keep your money. This is about love."

Love. A nebulous notion that he should understand but didn't.

With that one word, the atmosphere in the sunroom shifted, growing heavier with awareness. Her body leaned toward his, bristling with vibrancy. No longer poised to flee but to fight.

It reached out and punched him with a dark thrill. She wasn't backing down. She was prepared to meet him halfway, taking whatever he dished out. But what would she do with it?

"Hmm." The sound purred from his throat as he slanted her chin a touch higher. "Let's examine that. What do you know about love?"

More important, did she know the things he wanted to learn?

"I know enough," she retorted. "I know when I look at those babies, my heart feels as if it's about to explode with so many wonderful, terrible emotions. I know what it feels like to lose my sister to an early death and sob for days and days because I can't ever tell her I love her again."

Yes, that tightness in his chest when he'd gazed at his own flesh and blood encapsulated in a tiny person for the first time. It *was* wonderful and terrible. And inexplicably, that decided it. She was telling the truth about her motives, and all interest in grilling her over them evaporated.

Now his agenda included one thing and one thing only—Caitlyn and getting more of her soft skin under his fingers.

Love for a child he understood, but it wasn't the full extent of the kind of love possible. The kind of love he must have had for Vanessa. *That* was the concept that stayed maddeningly out of reach. "What about love for a man? Romantically."

"What, as if you're going to prove my motives are ugly because I've never been in love?" Fiercely, she eyed him. "I know how it feels to want a man to tell you he loves you. You want it so badly that you can't breathe. You want him to touch you and kiss you. It hurts deep down every second that you don't get it. And when you do get it, you want it to last forever."

Electricity arced between them and he ached to close the distance between them, to give her everything on her checklist, right here, right now.

"Is that what you wanted to hear?" she said, her chest rising and falling with quickened breath. "Love is equal parts need and commitment. What do *you* know about love?"

"Nothing," he growled, and instantly, the reality of it crushed through his chest.

The love that she'd painted with her impassioned speech—he wanted that. Wanted to know that he *could* feel like that. But love grew over time, over shared experiences, over shared memories.

He'd been robbed of that when he crashed in the ocean. But he had a chance to start over with someone else, to move on from the past he couldn't reclaim.

This nighttime interlude had started out as a way to get her to explain her motives, but instead, she'd uncovered his. Everything he wanted was right here, gripped in his hand. So he took it.

Hauling Caitlyn forward, he fused his mouth to hers. Hungrily, desperately, he kissed her, and his body ignited in a firestorm of sensation. Her mouth came alive under his, taking and giving with each stroke, matching him in the power of her appetite. He soared into the heavens in the most intense flight he'd ever experienced.

His eyes slammed shut as he savored the tight, heated pulls in his groin that could only be eased by burying himself in this woman, body and soul. *More.* He worked her mouth open and her tongue met his in the middle in a perfect, hot clash of flesh. Her eagerness coursed through him, spurring him on, begging him to take her deeper.

His mind drained of everything except her. He felt alive in the most elemental way, as if he'd been snatched from the jaws of hell for this moment, this woman.

Scrabbling for purchase, he slid his arms around her, aligning her with his body and dragging her into the most intimate of embraces. She clung to his shoulders and the contact sparked through his shirt. The contrast of her soft curves sliding against his brutally hardened torso and thighs drove him wild with sharp-edged need.

So frustrating. Too many clothes in the way. His fingertips explored her automatically, mindlessly, craving her. He wanted every millimeter of her beautiful skin exposed, wanted to taste it, feel it, rake it with his gaze and incite that gorgeous blush she could never seem to stop.

The kiss abruptly ended. Caitlyn tore out of his arms, hair in wild disarray from his questing fingers. Chest heaving, she stared at him, eyes limpid and heated.

And then she fled without a word.

* * *

Still mortified over her brazen behavior, Caitlyn curled in a ball on her bed, praying none of the babies would wake up tonight. Praying that Antonio didn't take her display of wantonness as an invitation to knock on her door. Because she didn't know if she'd open it. Or never come out.

She'd kissed her sister's husband. And the guilt was killing her—almost as much as the fact that she wouldn't stop herself from doing it again.

That kiss had rocked her to the core.

And shattered all her harmless fantasies about what it might be like to kiss Antonio.

The gap between imagination and reality was so wide, she couldn't see across it. Never would she have imagined her body capable of feeling such raw *need*. Or such a desire to let Antonio take her further into the descent of sensual pleasure, a place she'd never gone with any man.

The way he made her feel scared her, no doubt. But she scared herself even more. She was afraid of her own impaired judgment. If she gave in to that swirl of dark desire—which had seemed like a very real possibility when Antonio had taken her into his arms—what happened then? Was Antonio gearing up for a marriage proposal?

She had no idea how any of this worked. Where his thoughts were on the matter. How you even brought up such important subjects as commitment and love when a man had done nothing more than kiss you.

She needed these questions answered before she let these confusing new feelings brainwash her. The confusion was made even worse by the fact that it was *Antonio* on the other end of the equation. A different, harder, sexier, more over-the-top Antonio, who wasn't necessarily the man he'd been. She had no idea how to handle any of this.

And while she'd long ago accepted that she was already half in love with him, he hadn't professed any such thing to her. Sex was a big deal and until she knew he got that, no more kissing. Otherwise, she might find herself on the wrong side of a broken heart—as she'd always feared.

Along with a guilty conscience she couldn't shake, it was too much.

So they'd just have to pretend that scorching, mind-altering kiss had never happened.

By morning, she'd figured out that was impossible. The long, need-soaked night had not been kind.

Today's goal: get Antonio into a public place so he couldn't entice her again.

When he entered the breakfast nook, fresh from the shower, her heart did a crazy, erratic dance. It was sinful how perfect he was, how well his shoulders filled out a simple T-shirt, how his sinewy arms made her want to run her fingertips across them. Those arms... They'd held her expertly last night as he'd treated her to the most passionate kiss of her life.

How did the sight of him muddle her insides so much?

"Good morning," he murmured, his gaze full of knowledge.

"Hi," she squeaked in return. What did that dark, enigmatic look mean? That he remembered the taste of their kiss and wanted more?

Or was that a classic case of projection since that was what *she* was thinking? Would he even bring up the kiss, or was he of the same mind that it was better to forget about it?

Quickly, she tore her gaze from his and concentrated on her...oatmeal. At least that was what she vaguely recalled she'd been eating before he'd waltzed in and stolen her ability to use her brain.

"Would you like to go Christmas shopping with

me today?" she asked and winced at the desperation in the question. As if she was dying to spend the day in his company instead of the truth—public places were her new best friend.

He pursed his perfect lips, which made it really hard not to stare at them. *Oatmeal.* She put her head down and shoveled some in her mouth.

"I'd like that," he said easily. "Will we shop for the children? Or are they too young for gifts?"

"Oh, no. It's their first Christmas. I planned to shower them with presents and lots of brightly wrapped boxes. You know how kids only like to play with the boxes? I thought it would be fun to have empty boxes as well as toys. Of course, I came up with all of that before you returned, so if it's too extravagant—"

"Caitlyn."

She didn't look up. Didn't have to in order to know she was rambling again. Her name was like a code word. Anytime she heard it, it meant *shut up.*

With a soft rush of cloth, he crossed the breakfast nook, pausing by her chair. He tilted her chin to force her to meet his gaze. The way he'd done last night, but this morning, she didn't have the fuel of righteous indignation to keep her semisane. Caught in the grip of his powerful presence, she watched him, unable to look away or breathe. His fingers were like live electrical conduits, zapping her skin with energy, and she was pretty sure the heat had climbed into her cheeks.

"Let's just go shopping, okay?" he asked. "Money is not subject to discussion today."

"Oh. Um, really?" That certainly wasn't the tune he'd been singing last night. "I told you, I don't want your money, nor am I okay with treating you like a blank check."

She *had* said that, hadn't she? The atmosphere last night had been so vibrant and intense, there was no telling what she'd actually communicated now that she thought back.

"I believe you. So let's be clear. I'm paying. You are shopping." His smile broadened as she opened her mouth. "And not arguing," he added quickly before she could interrupt.

"So you don't have my name in your head next to a little check box labeled 'gold digger' anymore?" she asked suspiciously.

He shook his head and dropped his hand, which

she instantly wished he'd put back simply because she liked his touch.

"I'm sorry. I was less than tactful last night. We still have the future to sort out, but I'm less concerned about that today than I was yesterday. I'm willing to see what happens."

"You know I'm breast-feeding the babies, right?" she blurted out, and yeah, that heat was definitely in her cheeks.

His gaze narrowed, but to his credit, he didn't outwardly react to such an intimate topic. "All three of them?"

She scowled. "Yes, all three of them. Why in the world would I be selective?"

For some reason, that amused him. "I wasn't suggesting you should be. Forgive my surprise. It just seems like a huge undertaking. Though, admittedly, my understanding of the mechanics is limited."

Yeah, she'd bet he understood breasts better than most men. "It's a sacrifice, for sure, but one I'm more than willing to make. But the point is, I can't just stop. So there's not a lot of room for seeing how it goes. I'm their mother, not an employee."

He nodded. "I'm beginning to see that point more clearly."

At last. There was no telling if he'd actually softened his stance or whether she could explain her feelings any better now than she'd thus far been able to. But the time seemed right to try.

She shut her eyes for a beat and laid it on the line. "Well, thank you for that. You asked me last night what I envision and honestly, I see us co-parenting."

"You mean long-term?" Even that didn't ruffle his composure, which, hopefully, meant it wasn't too far out of a suggestion in his mind.

"Forever. They're my children," she said simply. "I want to shop for Annabelle's prom dress, see them graduate from college, be there when they get married. The works. There's not one single thing I'd agree to miss."

His silence wasn't very reassuring. Finally, he nodded once. "I don't know how to do that. But I'm willing to talk about it after the holidays, like we agreed. It will give us time to think about what that looks like."

Breath she hadn't realized she was holding whooshed out. It was something. Not the full-bore yes she'd have preferred but more than she'd had five minutes ago.

"That's great. Thank you. It means a lot to me."

"It means a lot to me that you're willing to be their mother." His dark, hooded expression sought hers and held again and she shivered under the intensity. "They need a mother. Who better than the one who carried them for nine months?"

"That's exactly what I've been trying to tell you," she said and wished she could have pulled that off with a smirk, but it probably just sounded grateful.

"Let me eat some breakfast and we'll go shopping." He smiled as Francesco hustled into the breakfast nook, carrying a bowl of oatmeal and some coffee with two teaspoons of sugar, milk and a shot of espresso, the way Antonio liked it.

Not that she'd memorized his likes and dislikes over the years, but she found it interesting that his coffee preference hadn't changed even through the nightmare of amnesia.

"I'll drive," she told him. "Unless your headache is better?"

"It's not as bad today." He glanced at her. "I

took a painkiller last night. Figured it was the only way I'd get to sleep after you ran out on me."

Amusement danced through his gaze along with a hint of heat that she had no trouble understanding. And on cue, there came the stupid blush. "I'm sorry. That was juvenile."

"Why did you take off, then?" Casually, he spooned up some oatmeal as if the answer didn't matter, but she caught the tightness around his mouth.

"It was too much," she said carefully. And honestly. "We have a lot of challenges in front of us. I'd like to focus on them without...complications."

That part wasn't the whole truth, but it was certainly true enough.

"That's a good point." Antonio polished off his breakfast without fanfare and without arguing.

Caitlyn frowned. Was she that easy to resist?

It didn't matter. No more kissing. That was the rule and she was sticking to it.

She stood and moved toward the door of the breakfast nook, hoping it didn't appear too much as if she was running away again, but Antonio confused her and she wanted to find a place where she could breathe for a few minutes. "I'll be ready to go shopping in about thirty minutes, if that's okay."

"Caitlyn."

She paused but didn't turn around.

"You focus on your challenges your way, and I'll focus on my challenges my way."

"What's that supposed to mean?" she whispered, afraid she wasn't going to like the answer.

"It means I'm going to kiss you again. The complications aren't great enough to stop me. You'd best think of another argument if you don't want me to."

Seven

The Malibu Country Mart at Christmastime might not have been the smartest choice for keeping her distance from Antonio. For the fourth time, the crush of holiday shoppers forced them together, and for the fourth time, his thigh brushed Caitlyn's hand.

She snatched it back before considering how telling a gesture it was.

Of course, his parting comment at breakfast had obviously been designed to throw her off balance, so alerting him to the fact that he'd succeeded shouldn't be that big of a deal.

"There's Toy Crazy," she squawked and cleared

her throat, pointing with her still-tingling finger. "Let's hit that first."

Antonio nodded without comment about her affected voice, bless him, and they walked in tandem to the store.

A Salvation Army bell ringer called out season's greetings as they passed, and the holiday decor added a cheerful mien to the shopping center that Caitlyn wished she could enjoy. She loved Christmas, loved the holiday spirit and had been looking forward to the babies' first experience with the festivities.

Now everything with Antonio was weird and uncertain and she hated that. For so long she'd dreamed of having a relationship with him, and nothing had happened like she would have thought. *He* was nothing like she would have thought, so different than the man he'd been before the crash. Darker, fiercer Antonio wasn't the tame businessman her sister had married, and Vanessa was far more suited to handle this version of the man than Caitlyn was.

Antonio had flat-out told her he was going to kiss her again. What did she do with that? How did she come up with a better argument than "It's complicated"? Especially when there wasn't a better argument.

"After you," Antonio murmured and allowed Caitlyn to enter the toy store ahead of him, then followed her closely as they wandered into the fray.

Dolls and rocking horses and toy trains dominated the floor space, jockeying for attention amidst the shoppers. Caitlyn grabbed a cart and jostled through the aisles in search of the perfect toys for their children. True to his words at breakfast, Antonio didn't allow her to look at prices, and insisted she put everything in the cart she wanted.

Somewhere along the way, the sensual tension faded and the task became fun. They were just two parents picking out presents for their kids: swapping suggestions, agreeing with each other's ideas, nixing the toys that one of them felt wasn't age appropriate—mostly Caitlyn took on that role, especially after Antonio joyfully picked out remote-control cars for Leon and Antonio Junior. Honestly. The boys couldn't even walk yet.

Before long, the cart overflowed and Caitlyn

had shared more smiles with Antonio than she'd expected, given yesterday's kiss.

"I don't think anything else will fit," she announced.

"Then, I suppose we're finished." Antonio nodded toward the front of the store. "Unless you want to get another cart and keep going."

She laughed. "No, I think this is enough to spoil three children rotten."

Antonio smiled and pushed the cart toward the register. He'd manhandled it away from Caitlyn about halfway through without asking, insisting it had grown too heavy for her to maneuver. How could she argue with chivalry?

After they paid and Caitlyn got over her sticker shock, she let Antonio carry the umpteen bags.

But she didn't make it two feet toward the door. Antonio nearly plowed into her when she stopped. 'Twas the season to spend money as if it was going out of style, but it was also the season to spread good cheer to those who wouldn't be waking up to their parents' overindulgence.

"I just remembered that I wanted to donate something to Toys for Tots." Caitlyn picked up a Barbie doll and a GI Joe action figure located near the register. "I'll pay for this out of my own money."

Antonio's brows drew together. "What's Toys for Tots?"

He didn't remember Toys for Tots? Amnesia was such a strange beast, constantly surprising her with the holes it had created in Antonio's mind. Her heart twisted anew as she imagined how difficult his daily life must still be.

"It's a charity sponsored by the US Marines that gives toys to underprivileged kids. Not everyone has a billionaire for a father," she joked. "I like to donate every year, but I selfishly got caught up in my own children this year and nearly forgot."

His expression flickered with a dozen inexplicable emotions.

"Wait here," he instructed. "I'll be right back."

Mystified, she watched him thread back through the crowd and say something to the girl behind the register. Wide-eyed, she nodded and called to another worker. They spoke furiously to each other and then the second worker came alongside the first to speak to Antonio. He handed her something and then returned to Caitlyn's side with a small smile.

"Sorry, but you can't use your own money to buy toys for the kids without fathers."

Kids without fathers. That wasn't what she'd said, but he'd interpreted the term *underprivileged* in a way that had affected him, obviously. And many of the Toys for Tots recipients probably *didn't* have fathers.

"Don't argue with me," she told him sternly. "I didn't say anything about you paying for the babies' gifts, but this is something for me to do on my own."

"I don't mean I don't want you to. I mean, you can't. I bought out the whole store," he explained, and didn't even have the grace to look chagrined.

"You...what?"

"I told the clerk that she should check out the people already in the store and I'd buy whatever was left." He looked downright gleeful. "So we're going to hang out until they clear the store and then she's going to run my credit card."

Her heart thumped strangely. "That's...extravagant. And generous. What brought that on?"

He shrugged. "I don't think I've ever done anything for others before. That charity event you mentioned, the one where I wore the pink shirt.

On the day we met," he prompted, as if she'd ever forget. "I did that because it was part of my contract. Not because I believed in the cause. I'm a father now. It means something to me and I want to be a better person than I was."

Tears pricked her eyes and she fought to keep them from falling. "You already are, Antonio."

Somehow her hand ended up in his and he squeezed it tight. "You're the one who brought it up."

What, as if she had something to do with Antonio's beautiful gesture? "Not so you could unload an entire toy store on the marines!"

He laughed and it rumbled through her warmly. *This* was what she'd dreamed of all those lonely nights when she imagined what it would be like to have a relationship with Antonio. Here they were, holding hands, standing near each other, and it was comfortable. Nice.

Not desperate and sensual and dark the way that kiss had been. Which one was the real Antonio?

His thumb stroked her knuckle and heat curled through her midsection. Okay, so he had the capacity to be both, which wasn't an easy thing to reconcile.

"I'll call someone to pick up the toys after the customers are gone and arrange for everything to be taken to the drop-off location," he said.

Yeah, there was nothing wrong with that part of his memory—he had no trouble recalling how to be large and in charge. And she hated that she found that shockingly attractive, too. As much as his generosity and his warrior-like persona and the way he was with the babies.

Who was she kidding? *All* of him was attractive.

When they got home, she spent an hour with the babies feeding them, which was time with her children that she treasured. They wouldn't breast-feed forever and while it had its challenges, such as having to use a breast pump after she'd had wine with Antonio the other night, she would be sad when this special bonding period was over.

Brigitte took over when Caitlyn was finished and they chatted for a few minutes. Leon was teething and making his displeasure known. Brigitte made a few suggestions and they agreed to try a different approach.

Should they include Antonio in discussions about the children's care? Caitlyn hadn't even thought to ask him but she really should. That was what being co-parents was all about.

She went in search of him and found him in his gym. Shirtless. And putting his hard body through a punishing round of inverted push-ups. Muscles bunched as he lowered himself to the ground and back up. His torso rippled and his skin glistened with his effort.

Dear Lord. A more exquisitely built man did not exist anywhere in the world.

Her mouth dried up. She couldn't peel her eyes from his body. Watching him put a burn in her core that ached with unfulfilled need. Somehow, the fact that he didn't know she was there heightened the experience, heating her further.

What was she *doing*?

She backed away, horrified to be gawking like a teenager. Horrified that she'd allowed herself to have a carnal reaction to Antonio.

"Caitlyn."

She glanced up. He'd climbed to his feet and stood watching her with a slightly amused expression. His torso heaved with exertion, and the falcon on his pectoral seemed poised to fly off his chest with each breath.

"Did you want something?" he asked, eyebrows raised.

So many things… "Uh—"

Wide-eyed, she watched him approach and speaking wasn't much of an option. His masculinity wrapped around her in a sensual cloak that settled heavily along her skin, warming it.

"Maybe you wanted to work out with me?" he asked, his head cocked in contemplation.

He was too close. Her body woke up in thrumming anticipation.

"I…um…do Pilates." *What did that have to do with anything, dummy?* She could still lift weights or something in Antonio's company, couldn't she? She shook her head. What was she thinking? That wasn't even why she'd tracked him down.

He reached out and toyed with a lock of her hair, smoothing it from her cheek, letting his fingers trail across her throat as he tucked the strand behind her back.

"Maybe you're here to deliver that argument we talked about earlier?" he murmured.

"Argument?"

Her mind went blank as Antonio's hand slipped from her shoulder to her waist. His naked chest was right there, within her reach. Her fingertips strained to trace the ink that bled into his skin, branding him as Falco. A fierce bird of prey.

"Against me kissing you. If you've got one, now would be the time to say your piece."

She glanced up into his eyes and the typhoon of desire swirling in their dark depths slammed through her. That sensual flare—it was desire *for her.*

She was his prey. She should be frightened. She was…and yet perversely curious what *would* happen next if she let things roll.

"We're, uh… That is…" She yelped as his arm slid around her waist, tugging her closer.

Her breasts brushed his bare torso, and even through her clothes, the contact ignited her already tingling core, flooding her with damp warmth.

"Caitlyn," he murmured. "Don't deny this. Hush now, and let me kiss you."

And before she could blink, he cupped her chin and lifted her head, bringing her mouth to his in one expert shot. The touch of his lips sang through her and she fell into Antonio, into the dark need, into her own pleasure.

Hot and hungry, he kissed her, hefting her deeper in his arms so their bodies snugged tight. She couldn't stop herself from spreading a palm on his heated flesh, right across his heart. Where the falcon lived.

His tongue coupled with hers, sliding against hers with rough insistence, and the sparks it generated ripped a moan from her throat.

Her core liquefied. No man had ever made her feel like this, so desperate and incomplete, as if she'd never be whole without him. She wanted… more. Wanted things she had little concept of. Wanted him to teach her about the pleasure she sought but hadn't yet realized.

Antonio gripped her shirt at the waist and pulled it from her pants before she could protest. Suddenly, his fingertips slid up her spine, magic against her bare flesh. She reveled in it, losing herself in his touch. He palmed her rib cage and thumbed one breast through her bra. Her core throbbed in time with her thundering pulse. Her head lolled backward as he mouthed down her throat to suck at the hollow of her shoulder blade, his unshaven jaw scrubbing her sensitive skin, heightening the pleasure tenfold.

That questing thumb worked its way under her bra and the shock of his rough, insistent touch against her nipple rocketed through her with a spike of dangerous lust.

"Antonio," she croaked and somehow got a grip on his wrist to pull it free from her clothing. "That's too far. It's too much. I can't—"

She bit off the rest—she sounded exactly like the inexperienced virgin she was. She peeled her hands from his chest and tore out of his grip.

"Don't run away," he commanded quietly. "Not this time. I enjoy kissing you. I want to make love to you. But you keep stopping me. Why?"

Afflicted, she stared at him, totally at a loss. "You want to…"

She couldn't even say that out loud. *He wanted to sleep with her.* Of course he did; she'd led him on like a wicked temptress who was perfectly prepared to strip naked right there in his gym and go at it on the floor.

This was her fault. She had no clue how to handle a man like Antonio, who was built like a woman's fantasy come to life. Who probably thought of sex as the next logical step in this type of attraction. No wonder she was screwing this up.

"I'm not like that," she said firmly. "I don't run around sleeping with people indiscriminately."

Something dangerous whipped through his expression. "I'm not 'people' and I object to being classified as such. You're cheapening what's happening between us. Also, I don't think that's the reason. You're afraid to be intimate with me."

He was offended. And disappointed in her. It scratched at her insides painfully. He'd cut through her surface protests to find the truth of her uncertainty. The realization that he understood her so well, even better than she'd understood her reticence, coated her throat, turning it raw.

"Yes," she whispered. "I need space."

She left the gym and he didn't try to stop her. Good. She needed to sort out her confusion. Antonio wasn't some random guy who'd love her and leave her, and of course he'd seen right through that excuse. Good grief, he had *commitment* written all over him—it was a huge part of his appeal.

Still was, but the physicality of her attraction far eclipsed it. Somehow. He'd brought out a part of her she'd never known existed. Around Antonio, she became a sensual, carnal woman that she didn't recognize, who liked his fierce side, his raw masculinity. Who wanted to delve into the pleasures of his touch with no regard to the emotional connection she thought she'd valued above anything else. And it scared her.

Because she didn't want to be like Vanessa. And yet, Caitlyn craved the type of relationship her sister had had with Antonio. It was a paradox, one she didn't know how to resolve.

Antonio had offered himself up on a silver platter. And she never dreamed she'd be fighting herself over whether to accept.

Antonio gave Caitlyn her space.

It was the last thing he wanted to do, but he had enough wits about him to recognize that Caitlyn required delicacy. Not his forte. But he'd learn it to get what he wanted.

The long night stretched, lonely and uncomfortable. The enormous four-poster bed would fit five people, but there was only one person he wanted in it. He had the vague sense that he must have slept in this bed with Vanessa, but he didn't think of his late wife at all. Instead, his vivid fantasies involved a dark-haired beauty who'd tied him up in knots.

Twice.

The first kiss had floored him. The second kiss had thrown him into a whole other level of senselessness. What had started as a way to help him move on from his marriage had exploded into something far more intriguing than he'd dreamed. When he kissed Caitlyn, her essence crawled inside him, haunting him. Pleasing and thrilling at the same time.

He wanted more. So much more. He shifted, unable to find a comfortable position, and the too-soft mattress doubled as a torture device. His half-aroused state didn't help.

The next morning, he bought a town car and hired a full-time driver to shuttle him back and forth to Falco. He still didn't feel comfortable driving, not with the headaches that sometimes cropped up out of the blue. Navigation sometimes tripped him up as well, especially while trying to get to a place he didn't remember. His house— no problem. Falco wasn't on the approved list of memories his brain had apparently created.

Fighting was his only outlet for the constant

frustrations. And his opportunities for it were limited.

Once at Falco, he first arranged for a private detective to start searching for the remaining two unaccounted-for passengers from his flight to Thailand. He gave the highly recommended man one instruction—spare no expense. If those two people were out there, Antonio would help them get back their lives.

Then he spent the afternoon with Thomas untangling legalities. They worked through the brunt of it until Antonio thought his head would explode with details and pain. This office job was where he belonged, where he'd built a company out of the ashes of his first love.

He didn't want it.

In reality, Antonio longed to climb back in the ring. The business side of this promotional venue he'd created didn't call to him as it once must have. Some aspects felt comfortable and familiar, though he didn't have conscious memories of strategy and balance sheets. Surely sitting behind his desk and monitoring his empire had once made him supremely happy.

As Thomas gathered up his paperwork, Antonio swiveled the high-backed chair toward the window, which overlooked a landscaped courtyard with a wishing-pool fountain in the center. He must have enjoyed this view often, as Caitlyn mentioned that he'd been a workaholic, often clocking eighty-hour weeks.

"Thomas, what would it take to get me back in rotation?" Antonio asked without taking his gaze off the gurgling fountain. Not only was it a shocking request in and of itself, but worse, the man who owned an MMA promotional company should probably know the answer already.

"You want to fight again?" Thomas kept any surprise from his tone, which Antonio appreciated. "As a contender? Or just exhibition?"

His mouth quirked involuntarily. "It's not worth doing if you're not going for the title."

The ins and outs of being a professional fighter he had no problems remembering. The pain and the training and the brutal conditioning…all worth it for a shot at glory.

But Antonio had underlying reasons. Reasons why he was a fighter in the first place. It was a part of him, an indelible piece of his makeup that even a near lobotomy of his memory couldn't extricate.

Thomas cleared his throat. "Well, you certainly proved the other day that you're in good enough shape for it. But you stopped fighting for a reason. What's changed?"

"*I* have. Make it happen."

After Thomas left, restlessness drove Antonio to the training facility, where several people called out greetings, none of whom he recognized, and without his mind-reading guide to assist, there was no chance he'd come up with names. If only Caitlyn hadn't requested her space, he'd have gladly brought her with him.

Trainers worked with fighters of all shapes and sizes, some in the rings, some at the bags. Along with the grunts and slaps of flesh, a sense of purpose permeated the atmosphere. Falco had been born out of Antonio's love of mixed martial arts, but he felt far more comfortable in this half of it than in the CEO's office.

He watched a couple of heavyweights duke it out in the circular-cage ring. Round, so one fighter couldn't force the other into an inescapable corner as so often happened in traditional boxing. MMA strove to even the playing field, to create fairness. The two heavyweights sparred under the watchful eye of a middle-aged man who moved with the fighters gracefully and knowledgeably. A former fighter, clearly, and Antonio liked his coaching style instantly.

Both men in the ring were good and they likely practiced together often. But one was better, with a stellar command of his body and a force of will the second man couldn't match.

Even without clear memories of planning or creating this place, Antonio recognized that he'd spared no expense when purchasing and maintaining the equipment. He'd also managed to attract world-class athletes and trainers, who'd sustained his company while he'd been in Indonesia.

Everyone here had come to improve their technique, to become better fighters, to win. Including Antonio. What happened in the ring made sense, followed a set of rules, a flow. The discipline and repetition settled him and allowed his damaged mind to take a breather.

"Who wants a piece of me?" he called.

"I'm up for it, if you are, old man."

Slowly, Antonio turned to face one of Thomas's right-hand men. A dark gray hoodie partially obscured the younger man's face, but his slight smirk beamed brightly from the depths.

The fighter vibrated with animosity, and Antonio's radar blipped. The man didn't like him. Dirty fight. Excellent. Darkness rose inside him and he didn't squelch it.

He'd been itching for this since his last round with Ravi in Punggur Besar. Rodrigo hadn't matched even a tenth of Antonio's skill and the fight had left him unsatisfied. Plus, Antonio and Rodrigo must have been friendly at some point in the past and that alone had caused Antonio to hold back.

There would be no holding back required with this matchup.

Antonio let his gaze travel down the length of his opponent and snorted his derision. "Hope your moves back up your mouth."

"Only one way to find out."

"What do they call you?" His real name was irrelevant, but the nicknames fighters adopted often gave clues about their style, their mind-set.

"Cutter." The insolent lift of his chin revealed

eyes so light blue, they were almost colorless. "Because you're gonna walk away with my cuts all over your face."

Or in some cases, when you were good at reading your competition, nicknames revealed their weaknesses. Cutter was arrogant. Overconfident. Eager to prove himself against the legendary Falco.

Of course, Antonio had known all of that the moment Cutter had labeled him "old man." And this punk was about to be schooled on what age meant for a man's technique and skill.

In minutes, Antonio and Cutter had suited up and squared off. Antonio sized him up quickly now that his opponent wasn't hiding under shapeless clothing. Muscular but not too bulky. Blond hair shaved close to his scalp. Viking-style tattoos across his torso and wrapped around his biceps. Feral sneer firmly in place. Nothing to differentiate him from the dozens of other fighters in his age and weight class—which was probably what pissed Cutter off the most.

The metal cage gleamed around them, providing a safe backdrop for the two men to tear each other up, no holds barred. No chance of being thrown from the ring…and no chance of escape.

There was nowhere to hide and nowhere to run. And blood would be spilled before long.

The younger man feinted and went low. Amateur. Antonio circled away and spun to catch him off guard with a sideways kick to his hip.

Cutter's retribution came in a series of attacks that kept Antonio busy deflecting. Duck. Spin. Feint. The rhythm became comfortable. Mindless.

In a split second, Antonio found a hole. *Attack.* His opponent was a lightweight, so Antonio had a few pounds on him, which he used ruthlessly to force Cutter against the fence. Going for the man's mouth was a no-brainer.

Antonio's fist connected and Cutter's flesh separated. The scent of blood rolled over him.

Cutter sprang forward with an amazing show of strength, fury lacing his expression and weighting his punches. A lucky cuff caught Antonio across the temple before he could block.

Pain exploded in his head, blurring his vision. Images of Vanessa's red hair ricocheted through his consciousness. Images of her in various scenarios. The two of them shouting at each other. Of her talking. Laughing. Of Antonio with her, skin bared, his hand on her flesh, mouth on hers.

Something about the memories pricked at him, sitting strangely. Something wasn't right. He couldn't—

He had no time to think.

Show no weakness. Blindly, he circled away, trying to give himself a moment to let his mind clear. The moment he regained his faculties, he went on the offensive. Uppercut, double kick. *No mercy.*

Often two fighters left the ring shaking hands. MMA was more gentlemanly than outsiders would assume. That wasn't the case in this ring.

In moments, it was finished. Antonio wiped the trickle of blood leaking into his right eye. Cutter lay crumpled on the mat, groaning.

Endorphins soared through his body like bullets. Memories of his wife crowded his mind. The metallic scent of blood stung his nose and he craved more.

"Anyone else want a go at me?" Antonio challenged.

No one volunteered.

Eight

Antonio sneaked into the house and closed himself off in his bedroom to clean up before anyone saw him. Anyone, meaning Caitlyn. The split skin near his eyebrow wasn't life threatening but it wasn't pretty, either. Nor was he good company, not with adrenaline still swirling through his body like a tornado.

A long, hot shower gave him decompression time, allowing him to force back the base urge to smack something again and again. Once he got going, it was hard to shut it off.

But he couldn't live in the ring. He had to find a balance between the need to fight and the rest of his life. Until he could, what kind of father would he be? How could he willingly expose his children to that?

Someone knocked on his bedroom door as he exited the bathroom, toweling off his damp hair. For modesty's sake, he draped the towel over his lower half and pulled open the door.

"Hi." Caitlyn's eyes strayed to his torso, lingered and cut back up again quickly. Pink bloomed in her cheeks.

He loved that blush, and with his body already caught in an adrenaline storm, it set off fireworks. His groin filled, primed for a whole different sort of one-on-one. Not a good combination when in the company of a woman who'd asked for space.

But then, she was also a woman who'd sought him out—in his bedroom. Maybe she'd gotten her space and was done with it.

Her eyebrows drew together as she focused on his face. "What happened? You're bleeding."

"I ran into something." He shrugged as her gaze narrowed. "Another guy's fist. I went to Falco this afternoon."

Her expression didn't change. "Do you need antiseptic? A Band-Aid?"

He bit back a smile. "No self-respecting fighter

walks around with a Band-Aid on his face. Thanks for the concern, but it doesn't hurt."

It didn't hurt because his body was still flying on a postmatch trip that ignored the pain of a cut. Instead, he was solely focused on the ache caused by Caitlyn's nearness. She was exactly what his queued-up body craved.

"Come in," he murmured thickly and held the door open wider.

She shook her head, eyes wide. "I don't think that's a good idea."

Oh, it was a very good idea. Obviously she thought so, too, or she wouldn't have knocked on his door. "Then, why *are* you here, Caitlyn?"

The question seemed to confuse her. She bit her lip and it drew his gaze to her mouth, causing him to imagine replacing her teeth with his.

She glanced away and cleared her throat. "I, uh, meant to talk to you about something, but I didn't realize you'd be…undressed."

"Didn't you?" He cocked his head. "That's what generally happens behind closed doors. Here, let me demonstrate."

But when he reached for the towel, intending to drop it and see where it led, she squeezed her eyelids shut. "No, no! That's okay. I get the point. I shouldn't have come to your bedroom, not after you'd just come back from Falco. I didn't realize you'd gone there, but you didn't come down for dinner, and I was worried and you're hurt and… this was a mistake."

Caitlyn whirled as if about to flee. Again.

Antonio shot out his hand to grip her arm before she took a step. "Caitlyn. Stop running away."

He needed her in a raw, elemental way. In other, more emotional ways he couldn't fully grasp. He didn't think it was one-sided, and the longer this back-and-forth went on, the clearer it became that they needed to deal with it head-on.

Smoothly, he turned her around to face him, searching her gaze for clues to her constant caginess. Confusion and something else skated through her expression.

"Come inside," he pleaded again.

If only he could get her on this side of the threshold, he'd feel less as if he was losing a grip on his sanity. If only he could get her to understand he was desperate to explore things he didn't fully grasp, things only she could teach him because she was the only woman he wanted.

"I can't." Her eyes were huge and troubled and her gaze flicked to the wound near his eyebrow. "I'm...scared."

The admission pinged through him, drawing blood with its claws of condemnation. He dropped his hand from her arm, flexing his raw fist, which smarted from connecting with bone in Cutter's face. Antonio lived and breathed to inflict bodily harm on other human beings, and she saw that about him.

She'd needed space because the falcon inside him frightened her. It *should* scare her.

He'd forced her to watch him fight the other day, forced her to remain in his presence now with evidence of his brutal nature plain as day on his face. Practically forced her into his room so he could have his carnal way with her because of his own selfish desires.

But she didn't leave when he let go. She had every right to. She deserved someone gentle and kind.

"I won't hurt you," he said brusquely, and cleared his throat. He'd done nothing to assure her otherwise. "I hate that you think I might."

Her rounded gaze flew to his and the glint of moisture nearly undid him.

"I'm not scared of *you*," she corrected, but her voice cracked halfway through. "Never of you. I…"

She swallowed and he watched the delicate muscles of her beautiful throat work. If she wasn't scared of him, what was it? And why was it so difficult for her to articulate?

"Then, tell me," he commanded softly, and reached out to grasp her hand in his so he could draw her forward. Almost over the threshold. She didn't resist, but neither did she rush. "What's going on in your mind when I do this?"

Slowly, he took her hand and placed it flat on his chest, over his thundering heart. Her touch nearly drove him to the carpet, but he locked his knees, sensing that if he could keep his wits about him, paradise might be within their reach.

Mute, she stared at her splayed hand under his. Her fingertips curled slightly as if she wanted to grip harder but couldn't.

"It's like granite," she whispered. "That's what I think about. So hard. But underneath lies something so amazing."

"What?"

"You. Antonio." His name fluttered from her throat on a half groan and the sound almost broke him open.

"You say that as if my name is poetry." It was just a simple name. But one he'd sought in the reaches of his messed-up mind for so long. Hearing it on her lips… It was an elemental thrill.

He was Antonio. And yet not. Because he couldn't fully remember all of the parts that created the whole.

"*All* of you is poetic," she murmured, and drew in a ragged breath. "The way you walk, the way you hold your children. How you move in the ring. I couldn't stop watching you and it was, um…nice."

"You liked watching me fight?" The idea was ludicrous. But her dreamy smile spoke volumes.

"I didn't think I would, but it was amazing." She sighed, a breathy sound that hardened him instantly. "Watching you execute those perfect moves, your body so fluid and in such harmony. It's like a perfect song lyric that when you hear it for the first time, it climbs inside your heart and lives there."

His own breath came more quickly as he stared at her with dawning comprehension. "You have feelings for me."

That was what he'd seen in her expression, what he couldn't quite grasp. It was a wondrous, blessed revelation. As obvious all at once as the sun bursting over the horizon to announce daytime. But he had no context for how he felt. And he wanted to.

Blinking slowly, she bit her lip again and nodded. "I've tried not to. But I can't help it."

A hundred questions rocketed through his mind, but he stuck with the most important.

"Then, why?" he asked hoarsely. "Why do you run away? Why are you so scared of what's happening?"

"I…" She glanced off and the moment of honesty, of her raw confession, started slipping away.

Desperate not to lose it, he cupped her face in both hands and brought it to his, a breath away. "What, Caitlyn? Tell me. Please. I'm losing my mind here. And I don't have much left to lose."

His wry joke earned him a watery smile.

"I'm scared of *me*," she whispered. "I want… things. Things I barely understand. It's like in all the fairy tales where they tell the girl not to touch the spindle or not to eat the apple. I never understood why they couldn't help themselves. Because I never understood what it meant to truly *desire* something. Or someone. Until you. I don't know what to do."

She wanted him. And that made all the difference.

"There's only one right answer to that."

He leaned into the space between them and laid his lips on hers for a scant second, kissing her with only a thousandth of the passion he wished he could unleash. But didn't because she wasn't fully inside the room.

Once she stepped over the threshold, all bets were off.

Pulling back with an iron will that could only be developed by years of ruthless training, he evaluated her. "Do you like kissing me?"

"Yes," she murmured. "More than I should."

"Then, come inside. Let me kiss you. Let me give you that experience you described. Let me be the man who touches you and loves you."

He wanted that—badly. Wanted to feel her skin next to his, to feel alive alongside her. To feel as if the things she spoke of were more than just words but concepts his soul recognized.

Her eyes closed and her lips pursed as if in invitation, as if she yearned for him to kiss her again. But then her eyes blinked open and she swallowed. Hard.

"I need to tell you something else." Her gaze sought his and held. "I've never had a lover before."

Antonio's expression didn't waver, bless him. "You're a virgin?"

Caitlyn nodded. Her tongue was stuck to the roof of her mouth, glued there by nerves and who knew what else—three or four of the seven deadly sins, most likely.

"That explains a lot. I'm sorry you didn't trust me with that fact sooner. That's why you asked for space." His chiseled lips turned down. "I didn't give it to you."

Her heart fluttered. Antonio had the patience of Job.

"You did," she corrected hurriedly. "You've been perfect. I'm the problem. That's what I've been trying to tell you. I don't have any experience at…you know. And I'm nervous. You're this beautiful, wonderful man with all these expectations about being with me, probably because I've led you on, and I'm… Well, I'm not Vanessa, that's for sure—"

"Caitlyn." The quirk of his eyebrow rendered her speechless, as he'd probably intended. "Are you trying to tell me that you think I'll compare you unfavorably to Vanessa?"

"Uh…" Clearly, yes wasn't the right answer. But it was the only one she had. "She was so gorgeous, with a body men salivated over. She knew how to please a man in bed, too, which she liked to brag about. It's hard to imagine following that."

His quick smile knocked her off-kilter. Was it *that* funny?

"Isn't it ironic, then," he mused, "that I can't remember Vanessa?"

"At all?" He couldn't remember his wife, the one he'd ended his career for, whose babies he'd wanted to have so badly, he'd agreed to surrogacy?

Her gaze flicked to the year-old scar disappearing into his hairline. What kind of whack to the head had he endured that his memories were that insubstantial? It must have been vicious.

"Some." His tone grew somber. "I see flashes of her red hair and remember bits and pieces, like her laugh. It's all jumbled in my head. Sometimes it's her face and sometimes her body. But I don't remember being in love with her. I feel so disconnected from her, as if she wasn't real. I don't remember feeling like you said I should, as if I want to be with her so badly I can't breathe."

The despondency in his voice caught in her chest and made it hurt. "I'm sorry, Antonio. I didn't realize you hadn't regained your memories of her. That must be very difficult."

"What's difficult is that I want to move on." His lashes lowered and he speared her with that dark, enigmatic glance that set her blood on low simmer. "I want to be in the here and now, not stuck dwelling on the past I can't remember. I've found someone new, someone I *do* want so badly I can't breathe. I want to love her and fulfill her and let her do the same to me. But I can't seem to get her into my arms."

"Me?" she whispered.

Heat climbed into her cheeks, on cue. *Duh*. Of

course he meant her. But her brain wasn't working quite right. Too busy filtering through the divine idea that Antonio wanted to love her.

"Yes, you." His thumb feathered across her hot cheek. "I not only can't compare you to Vanessa, I don't want to. I want what's possible now, for as long as we have together. I want to learn about the kind of love that you talked about. Teach me."

"How can I teach you anything? I'm not the one with experience."

His gorgeous lips turned upward into a killer smile. "I'm not the one with any experience I can remember. In a way, this will be the first time for both of us."

For some reason, that appealed to her. Immensely.

He didn't remember Vanessa and wanted to learn everything about love, sex, relationships over again. It was like the slate being wiped clean—Caitlyn could make this experience anything and everything she could imagine, be as wicked in his arms as she wished and wrap it up in a beautiful emotional connection that could last an eternity.

He'd come back from the dead a different person, and she'd often dwelt on the darker changes. It had never occurred to her that amnesia would be a positive in this one case.

Except he'd been born with a body designed for pleasure, and just as he'd not forgotten how to breathe, he likely hadn't lost any knowledge of how to make a woman quiver with desire. She couldn't do the same to him, no way.

"Are you sure this is what you want? With me? I mean, you might not precisely remember Vanessa, but you have to recall other women." *Shut up.* Nobody brought up former lovers on the brink of becoming the next one. She sighed. "See. I'm a big mess. That's so not attractive, I realize."

He glanced down at the two feet of space between them. "We've been standing in this doorway for ten minutes now, and for nine minutes and fifty-five seconds of it, I've been in danger of losing this towel due to the serious arousal you've caused me. Stop worrying so much about things that don't matter. Don't deny us any longer, Caitlyn."

He stepped aside, opening the doorway for her to enter if she chose.

This was it. Her opportunity to grab what she'd

longed for. To put her guilt to rest and finally become a full-fledged, sexually realized woman at the hands of a master. A man who was probably the great love of her life, the only one she might ever love.

And his pretty speech about learning how to love at *her* hands surely meant he was open and willing to returning her feelings. He'd loved Vanessa, had married her and obviously yearned to have that sort of connection again. The sort of connection Caitlyn had dreamed of.

It was all within her reach.

Yet she hesitated, long enough for his eyebrows to rise.

What would happen if she stepped over the threshold, signaling to Antonio that she was ready to embark on a romantic relationship, and if it didn't work out? How would she co-parent their children with a broken heart? The past few years had been difficult enough when she'd revered him from afar. How much harder would it be to actually love and be loved by a man like Antonio, only to lose him because she wasn't the kind of woman who could handle him?

And what if he cut her out of her children's lives in retribution?

This was why she never got very far in a relationship with any man, including Antonio when she'd first met him. She was terrified of what came *after* she opened herself body and soul to someone.

As she let her gaze rest on his bare torso, on that glorious inked falcon, she wanted to let him melt her resistance.

Because it would be impossible to walk away.

She took a breath to calm her racing heart, which didn't work, and walked into Antonio's bedroom.

Nine

The door clicked shut behind her and Caitlyn froze.

She was inside a man's bedroom. She wouldn't leave it a virgin. She'd been saving herself for the right man, a man she was ready, willing and eager to love forever, and here he was...but this wasn't the safe fantasy she'd harbored for years. Was she *really* ready for this?

Oh, my. Antonio was going to see her naked, with her C-section scars and ridiculously shaped breasts that had served as a milk source for three hungry mouths for months.

Nearing full-blown panic, she tried to suck in a deep, calming breath. And choked on it as she thought back to getting dressed this morning. What underwear had she put on?

"Caitlyn."

She whirled. Antonio leaned against the door, arms crossed over his cut torso, towel dipping dangerously low. Her mouth went sticky and she averted her gaze. Then shifted her gaze back because, dang it, *surely* it was okay to look at him if they were about to make love. Maybe it was even expected. Part of foreplay.

"Do you want a glass of wine?" he asked casually.

"To drink?" When he laughed, she thought about punching him but would probably only hurt her hand. Mortified, she scowled. "I didn't know what you meant! Maybe it's some kind of sex thing, like you want me to pour it on you and lick it off."

His eyebrows rose and he treated her to a thoroughly wicked once-over. "Would you? Lick it off?"

The image of her tongue swirling over the ink on his chest popped into her mind and she couldn't shake it. As she imagined the taste of his golden skin melded with fruity red wine, her insides contracted. "Maybe. *Was* it a sex thing?"

He shrugged, a smile still playing about his expressive mouth. "As much as I want you right now, it could be. Seems a little messy, though. Let's save that for another time."

"How many times do you envision there being?"

"A thousand." His expression darkened carnally as if he was imagining each time individually and it was hot. "The things I want to do to you, to experience with you, might very well take a lifetime."

She couldn't blink, couldn't look away. Couldn't quite believe the sincerity ringing from his voice. She rubbed at the ache in her chest as she internalized that she'd heard precisely what he'd meant for her to hear. "A lifetime?"

Of course, it was what she'd yearned for. But it was another thing entirely to hear it from Antonio's mouth.

He tilted his head quizzically. "You aren't the kind of person who sleeps around indiscriminately. Neither am I. I want to be with you from now on. Awake, asleep. In bed, out of bed. Which part is confusing you?"

"All of it. Starting with 'hi' when I first knocked on the door," she muttered.

"So that wasn't a good subject, obviously. Here's what we're going to do instead," he said decisively, because of course he could read her like a book. "We're going to have a glass of wine. Then we're going to take this as slowly as you want to."

"Why?" Could she have sounded more suspicious? He was saying all the right things and she was botching this.

"The wine is to relax you," he explained, not seeming at all bothered by her lack of decorum. "Actually, both parts are to relax you. And both parts get me where I want to be. Inside you. Anticipation will make it sweeter, so I'm quite happy with the idea of taking my time. I've got a whole night and I'm not afraid to use it."

Dumbfounded, she let him lead her to his sitting area overlooking the coastline and sank onto the love seat he pointed to. Apparently, Antonio was botchproof. Good thing. She'd probably do ten more things to increase her mortification level before the night was through.

He selected a bottle of red wine from the rack on the wet bar and pulled the cork. Since his back was to her, she watched his bare torso unashamedly. Too quickly, he returned with two glasses full of deep red wine, handed her one and settled in next to her on the love seat. Clad in a towel.

It should be weird. He was completely naked underneath the terry cloth, which gaped at his thigh, revealing the muscular stretch of leg that led to his…good parts.

He glanced at her and then followed her line of vision. "Curious?"

Yes, wine was a fantastic idea. The alcohol needed to be swimming through her bloodstream, not sitting in a glass untouched. She gulped as much as she could get down, for fortification.

Because, oh, yes, she was curious. Burning with it.

"I've never seen a naked man before," she croaked.

Not enough wine, obviously, if she was still going to utter gems like that.

"Not even in pictures?"

She shook her head. "I'm a novice. I tried to tell you."

Antonio set down his glass on the side table with a hard click and then took her free hand in his. "Listen to me, because I don't want there to be any confusion about this."

Heart hammering in her throat, she stared at him as something tender sprang into his gaze.

"It means everything to me that no other man has ever touched you. That I get to be the first. It's an honor and I intend to treat it as such. You should never feel as if you have to apologize for this gift you're giving me."

"I…um." What did you say that *that*? "Okay."

That must have been the magic word. His thumb brushed over her knuckles and he let go of her hand to run his fingertips over the back of her wrist.

And kept going up her bare arm, watching her with that dark intensity as he touched her. Without a word, he took the glass from her suddenly nerveless fingers and set it next to his. A breath later, his mouth descended and took hers in a slow, deliberate kiss that melted her bones.

His sweet lips… They molded hers, explored. Slowly, as promised.

"Wait," he murmured, and his heat left her as he rose to click off the lights. Moonlight poured in from outside the glass, illuminating the love seat and throwing the rest of the room into shadow.

Antonio returned with the comforter from his bed and a couple of small squares that she eyed curiously until she realized what they were. Condoms. This had just turned real and her throat closed.

He spread the comforter in front of the floor-to-ceiling window and stretched out on it, beckoning her to join him. "Just to set the mood."

But the sight of Antonio bathed in the glow from the moon froze her completely. He was beautiful, mystical. Too perfect to be real. She just wanted to soak him in, to gorge herself on his splendor.

He seemed to sense her thoughts and lay still, allowing her to gaze at him as much as she wanted. The scar marking the location of his once-broken leg forked up his calf, as seductively savage as the rest of him.

After an eternity, he reached for his towel and held it in both hands, poised to take it off. "Do you want to see all of me?"

Too numb to speak, she nodded, but before she could properly school her expression or her thoughts or her...anything, the towel fell away and... *Oh, my*. He was utterly divine in all his glory, hard everywhere, with a jutting erection she'd felt when he'd kissed her in the gym, but never in a million years would she have thought it would look like *that*.

She couldn't stop drinking him in. And he didn't seem to be in a hurry to stop her.

"By the way," he murmured, "you know you're going to do this for me in a minute, right?"

"Do what?" Then she clued in. "You mean lie in front of the window naked so you can stare at me?"

A wolfish smile bloomed on his face. "Let me know when you're ready."

"I don't think I'll ever be ready for that," she muttered.

He flipped onto his hands and knees and crawled to her, kneeling between her legs. "Then, I'll have to fix that. Because I want to see you in the moonlight. I want to watch your face as I make love to you. And you will most definitely need to be naked for that."

With exquisite care, he cupped her face with both hands and brought her lips to his.

This kiss was nothing like the one a minute ago, when there'd still been a towel and some modesty between them. There was nothing but Antonio between her legs, and when his mouth claimed hers in a scorching kiss, he palmed the small of her back and shoved her to the edge of the couch, almost flush with his body. Close, so close, and she arched involuntarily, seeking his heat.

His tongue plunged toward hers, possessing her with his taste, with his intoxicating desire. Moaning, she slid her arms around his strong torso, reveling in the feel of his sleek, heated skin under her palms. A small movement forward, just the slightest tilt of her hips, and his erection would brush her center.

And she ached for that contact. Desire emboldened her and she strained for it.

When it came, she gasped. He must have sensed her instant need for more because he pressed harder, rubbing in small circles. Heat exploded at her core and her head tipped back in shock.

He followed the line of her throat with his luscious lips, laving the tender skin expertly until he got a mouthful of her blouse. She nearly wept as his mouth lifted.

"I'm going to take this off," he murmured and fingered the first button for emphasis. "Okay?"

She nodded, appreciative that he respected her nerves enough to ask. Plus, she was very interested in getting his magic mouth back on her skin. "Seems fair. You're not wearing a shirt."

His warm chuckle had a hint of wicked that shuddered through her. Now, *that* was delightful.

"I'm not wearing anything. If you want to talk about fair…"

"You know what, you're right."

This imbalance *wasn't* fair. She stood quickly without thought of his proximity, and it was a testament to his superior balance that she didn't bowl him over.

He sat back on his muscular haunches, completely at ease in his own skin. She wanted to be that confident. To feel as if she belonged here, able to handle a man as virile and gorgeous as Antonio. There was only one way. She had to get over this virgin hump and take this night— her destiny, her *pleasure*—into her own hands. It wasn't Antonio's job to lead her through this.

He desired her. It was in his expression, in his words. In the hard flesh at his center. What purpose did it serve to protect her maidenly modesty? None.

She wanted him to take her in the basest sense. *Now.* And she wanted it to be hot. Sinful. Explosive. He could make that happen, she had no doubt. But he was holding back. She could feel it.

"I'm ready," she announced, and though her hands shook, she slipped the first button on her blouse from its mooring.

His eyelids lowered a touch as he watched her move on to the next button. "Ready?"

Third button. Fourth. "For you to see me. In the moonlight."

Heat flared in his expression and he hummed his approval. The sexy sound empowered her. Last button.

She slipped the blouse from her frame, gaze glued to his, and let it float from her fingers. That wasn't so bad. The clasp on her bra was a little harder to undo even though it was in front, and she couldn't even blame that on being a novice; she'd definitely taken her bra off a million times in her life, but never in front of a man, and this was it—the first time a man would see her bare breasts—and suddenly, the clasp came apart in her hands.

Well, that was the point, wasn't it?

Nothing left to do but shed the hideous nursing bra. In retrospect, stripping out of it probably increased her sexiness quotient. She dropped it on the ground near her blouse and fought the urge to cover herself when Antonio's heavy-lidded gaze swept her with clear appreciation.

"You might want to hurry," he muttered, hands clenched on his thighs as he looked up at her from his prone position. "I'm about to lose my mind."

"Really?" That sounded...lovely. "Am I making you crazy?"

The thought pleased her. Imagine. Caitlyn Hopewell was driving a man insane with a slow striptease. It practically made her giddy.

He groaned. "Completely. You're killing me. If you had any idea how much I want to—" He shook his head, teeth gritted. "Never mind. You take this at your pace. I'll be the one over here practicing my patience."

"No. Tell me. What do you want to do?" She fingered the clasp on her jeans, toying with it the way she imagined a more experienced woman might do. "I might let you."

"Oh, yeah?" he growled. "Lose those pants and let's rumble, my darling."

The endearment rolled through her and left a whole lot of heat and pleasure in its wake. "I like it when you talk to me like that."

"You do, huh?" Amusement curled his lips upward. "Not well enough, since you're still dressed."

"Well, you still haven't told me what you want to do." The curiosity was killing her. So she shoved off her pants, careful to take her non-sexy underwear along for the ride, and kicked them both away.

She couldn't get more naked. With the moon as the only source of light, her flaws weren't as noticeable and the lines of her postpregnancy body smoothed out. And that was when it dawned on her—that had been the whole purpose of lights-out. Was there nothing that the man missed?

Antonio worshipped her with his gaze and she let him, keeping her arms by her sides. The way he looked at her made her feel beautiful. As though she had nothing to hide.

"Now then. Tell me," she commanded, proud that her voice didn't waver. "What sorts of wicked activities do you have in store? Because I've waited a lifetime to be thoroughly ravished and I'm a little anxious to get started."

Groaning, Antonio tried to keep his faculties about him as he surveyed the very tempting woman on display before him wearing nothing but moonlight and a smile.

Blood and adrenaline pounded through his veins. He'd kept a very tight hold on his body since he'd opened the bedroom door. Caitlyn had just pushed him to the brink with a unique mix of innocence and friskiness that belied her lack of experience.

He hadn't expected it to be such a turn-on.

Or for her to systematically break down his resistance until he held on to his self-control by the barest edge. He wanted her more fiercely than he'd ever wanted anything—including his memories. His muscles strained to pounce. To possess. To claim. To relentlessly drive her to the threshold of madness the way she'd driven him.

But he couldn't because Caitlyn deserved something special for her first time. She deserved someone gentle. Restrained. Refined.

She had to make do with Antonio Cavallari instead.

"I..." He nearly swallowed his tongue as Caitlyn sauntered toward him, invitation in her eyes that he couldn't misread even in the pale light. "My intentions are to make love to you. There's nothing wicked about that."

The hard floor beneath the comforter ground into his knees, but he couldn't have moved if his life depended on it. He should have prepared better for this, changed out the furniture. Caitlyn's first experience with sex should happen in a bed, but he refused to make love to her in the same place he'd been with another woman. Whether he could remember it or not. It was a matter of principle.

"Why not? What if I want wicked?" she murmured and halted directly in front of him, then folded her legs under her to mirror his pose. Knee to knee. She pierced him with a gaze far too knowing for a woman of her innocence. "Listen to me so there's no confusion about this, Antonio. I watched you in the ring and it was brutal.

But it was beautiful at the same time. Like you. It was an unsettling, thrilling experience. There's probably something wrong with me that I like the primal part of you. But I don't care."

Without hesitation, she traced the falcon tearing across his flesh, watching him as she touched him, and he sucked in a breath as his skin pulsed under her fingers.

"I want Falco," she said simply. "And Antonio. I'll only have one first time. Make it memorable. Give me all of it and don't hold back."

His iron will dissolved under the onslaught of her sensuous plea. With equal parts desperation and need, he hauled her into his arms and fell into her, into the innocence that called to him. Not to destroy, but to absorb. She was perfectly whole and exquisite and the shattered pieces of his soul cried out for her.

Hungrily, he kissed her, twining her body with his so he could feel her. His skin screamed for more of the sweet friction against hers. He palmed her heavy breasts, which filled his hands and then some. They were gorgeous, full, with huge nipples that his mouth strained to taste.

Unable to wait, he sucked one between his lips.

She gasped and her back arched instantly. *Yes.* Amazingly responsive, as he'd fantasized. He moved to the other breast, and the sensation of his tongue curling around her hard nipple had him pulsing with need.

The groan ripped from his throat and he murmured her name as he eased her back against the comforter. Moonlight played with her features as she lay there, exactly as he'd envisioned, and it was almost too much to take in. The mother of his children. His savior. Soon to be lover.

He needed her. Needed to be inside her, with her, loving her. But first things first. He bent one of her legs back and knelt to swirl his tongue at her center.

She froze and made mewling sounds in her throat.

"Shh, my darling," he murmured and kissed her inner thigh. "You asked for wicked." He kissed the other and opened her legs farther. "Close your eyes and imagine me in the ring. What about it excited you?"

"You were so graceful," she murmured. "Like an apparition. But so very real and raw. It made me hot. All over."

"Like this?"

Slowly, he touched her again with the tip of his tongue. She shuddered but didn't tense up this time. He went a little farther, lapping a little harder. Her hips rolled and she sighed in pleasure.

"That's right, sweetheart. Lie still, think about me and let me taste you." He cupped her hips and tilted her up to his lips to feast.

She thrashed under his onslaught, but since her shudders brought her center closer and closer each time, he took full advantage of it instead of scolding her for doing the opposite of lying still. Honey gathered under his tongue a moment before she cried out.

Her climax went on and on and his own body throbbed in response, aching for a release in kind inside this woman.

Shaking with the effort, he managed to roll on a condom without breaking it—a minor miracle, given that he couldn't precisely remember the technique—and stretched out next to her to take her into his arms.

"Ready?" he asked hoarsely, shocked he could speak at all.

"There's more?" Since the question was laced

with wry humor, he hoped that meant she was kidding.

"Oh, yes, there's more," he said fiercely. "I'm dying to show you."

She feathered a thumb across his lips, sparking sensation to the point of pain. "Show me, Antonio."

More roughly than he'd intended, he nudged a knee between her thighs and rolled, poised to thrust with all his pent-up energy. But he held back at the last second, somehow, and kissed her with every ounce of that longing instead. When she responded with a throaty moan that he felt in his groin, he couldn't wait. He pushed as slowly as he could into her center.

She wasn't on board with slow.

Her hips rose up to meet him, accepting him, encouraging him, and with a groan, he sheathed himself completely. Then forced his muscles to pause, though every fiber of his being screamed to let loose, to drive them both to completion with frenzied coupling.

He sought her gaze. "Tell me it's okay."

She nodded and let out a breath, her eyes shining as she peered up at him, hair a dark mass around her ethereal face. *She* was the apparition, a heavenly body trapped on this plane, and he'd been lucky enough to find her.

"It doesn't feel like I would have thought," she commented.

That made two of them.

Emotion he couldn't name wrenched at his heart, threatening to pull it from his chest. *Love.* He wanted it to be love, to know that he could feel such things and wasn't irreparably damaged.

But the sense he had of his previous experiences didn't match this. Not even close. This was so much bigger, so overwhelming. What if he *was* damaged? What if his memories never returned? How would he know if he was loving Caitlyn the way she deserved?

"You feel amazing," she murmured. Experimentally, she wiggled her hips. "What does it feel like to you?"

Her innocent movements set off a riptide of heat. "Let's compare notes later."

Settling her firmly under him, he began to move, rendering them both speechless. She arched against him, nails biting into his shoulders, those perfect, full breasts peaked against his torso.

Thrust for thrust, she met him, never retreating, never yielding. *More. Faster.* His body took from hers and she gave endlessly. Palming her rear, he changed the angle. Reversed the dynamic so he was doing the giving. Spiraling her higher into the heavens where she'd already taken him.

He needed to discharge, to explode. But he couldn't...not yet. He tasted blood on his lip where he'd bitten down with the effort to hold back. Animalistic sounds growled from his throat as he bent one of her legs back to go deeper still.

Exquisite pleasure rolled over him, and he needed more. Relentlessly, he rolled his hips to meet hers, and when she tightened around him with a small moan, he lost control.

Groaning as he spilled his release, he collapsed to the side, rolling her with him as he lost all feeling in his extremities.

In the aftermath, they lay together, and he gently spooned her into his body to hold her tightly. She snuggled in willingly with a small sigh of contentment.

He let her essence bleed through him as he lay with his eyes shut, absorbing her. If he never had to move from this spot, it would be too soon.

An instant later, he cursed his own selfishness. "Can I get you anything?"

What did you give a woman who had just offered up her virginity? Diamond earrings? A washcloth? She was likely bruised and raw. It wasn't as if he'd been gentle, not the way he'd pretended he was going to be.

"I'm fine, thanks. Don't you dare move." She wiggled closer to him. "Your body heat feels good against my sore muscles."

"I should have gone slower." Remorse crashed through his breastbone. He'd taken her innocence like the brute that he was. "I'm sorry I hurt you."

"Don't you dare apologize. Some of it hurt, but in a good way. It was amazing. Perfect. Beautiful. Everything I've ever dreamed of." Threading her fingers through his, she raised his hand to her lips. "Thank you for that."

Emotion clogged his throat and he swallowed against it, fighting to keep himself level.

The things she made him feel… He wished he could understand them. Could draw on his past to make sense of the swirl in his belly when he looked at her. But he couldn't.

All he knew was that Caitlyn was a miracle.

Everything he'd prayed to find when he'd set off from Indonesia in search of his life.

He stroked her side and with moonlight spilling over them both, he murmured the million-dollar question. "Why me? Of all the men in the world you could have chosen for your first experience."

"I always wanted it to be you," she said slowly. "Well, not *always*. Vanessa was…rather free with her affections, even back in high school. I didn't like how broken up she always was after, and I vowed to save myself for the right man. The first moment I met you, I had this strange shock of recognition, like *there you are*."

His hand stilled. "The first moment? You mean the pink-shirt meeting?"

She nodded and her hair brushed his chin. "After that, no other man could compare. I've had a crush on you for a long time."

"Even while I was married?" It should have seemed wrong, but it thrilled him for some reason. Caitlyn had been saving herself for *him*, even through his marriage to someone else. It spoke to her constancy and devotion, and it humbled him.

"I didn't say I was a saint. I had a lot of mixed feelings about it. You know, I cried for almost two days straight when they came to tell me the plane had crashed. I thought I'd lost you forever," she whispered brokenly.

In the long pause, he gathered her in his arms and held her as close as physically possible as his heart thumped in tandem with hers.

While he'd been lost and alone, Caitlyn had been here in his house, mourning him. He'd thought no one cared. But she had. She still did.

It was a far better gift than her virginity.

Ten

The next morning, Caitlyn awoke at dawn, stiff and sore from a night sleeping on the floor entwined with Antonio. And every inch of her body felt glorious.

Antonio had kissed her soundly before sending her off to her own room, presumably to keep the rest of the household in the dark about the new relationship that had bloomed between them. She showered under the hottest stream of water she could stand, letting the water ease her aches. Her thoughts never strayed far from the sexy man down the hall.

He might even be in his own shower, naked, with water sluicing down his gorgeous body. Feeling a little scandalous, she allowed the image to play through her mind...because she could. She knew what every inch of that man's flesh looked like, thank you very much.

She'd slept with Antonio. Her sister's husband, whom she had always coveted. There was probably a special place in hell for a woman who did that. And she hated to admit that she'd loved every second of it.

When she emerged, steam had obscured the mirror. She wiped it with a towel and stared at herself in the glass. Odd. She didn't look any different than she had yesterday morning, and it was a bit of a shock to see her same face reflected back at her.

By all rights, there should be *some* external mark to account for the rite of passage she'd undertaken. What, she couldn't say. But a man had loved her thoroughly last night. He'd filled her body with his, tasted her intimately, brought her to a shuddering climax. Twice. It was an earthshaking event worthy of distinction. Maybe she should get a tattoo to commemorate the experience.

A dove on her breast, maybe.

Silly. She was already picking out matching tattoos after sleeping with a man one night.

But it had been so incredible. Now she totally got why he'd said he planned to do it a thousand more times. Once could never be enough.

She'd just pretend he'd never been married to Vanessa. Block it out and never think about it. Vanessa was gone, and Caitlyn and Antonio deserved to move on. Together. It wasn't a crime.

At breakfast, the babies played with their bananas and Cheerios as always, Brigitte chattered up a storm as she did every morning and Caitlyn sat in her usual spot at the table. But the secret looks Antonio shot her gave everything a rosy, sensual glow, and she was very much afraid she was grinning at him like a besotted fool.

Perhaps she should be more covert if the goal was to keep their relationship on the down low.

"Caitlyn and I are going shopping today," Antonio announced out of the blue when everyone finished eating.

"We are?" Did they have some Christmas presents to buy that she'd forgotten about? "It's two days until Christmas. The stores will be insane."

"I believe I have adequately demonstrated my

ability to dispense with holiday crowds," he countered with a smirk.

"So that's your solution to everything now? Just
buy out the whole store?"

"When I find something that works, I stick with
it. You might consider thanking me for that." His
dark gaze flickered with promise, and yesterday,
such innuendo might have made her blush, but
she was a worldly woman now. So she stuck her
tongue out at him instead.

Brigitte watched all of this with unabashed fas-
cination, probably interpreting the exchange in
the wrong way. "Well. You two have *fun*."

Or the right way, depending on how you looked
at it.

Antonio herded her into the Range Rover, and
she dutifully drove, navigating through the paparazzi outside the gate. She wasn't used to all
of this. The cameras had camped out there ever
since the first time Antonio had gone to Falco.

As always, Antonio ignored them. Oh, his lawyer and Thomas Warren had fielded a ton of questions on Antonio's behalf, but he wasn't in a hurry
to take that part of his life back. He liked his privacy, which suited Caitlyn fine.

Once they were clear of the knot of people and vans, she asked, "What are we shopping for?"

"Bedroom furniture."

She glanced at him askance and flicked her gaze back to the road immediately. "Because there's something wrong with the furniture you already have?"

"Yes. It's Vanessa's," he explained quietly, oblivious of the sword he'd just stuck through her abdomen. "Every stick of furniture in that room will be gone by the time we return. I already arranged it. Help me pick out something new."

Oh. So that was why they'd slept on the floor. He didn't want to sleep with Caitlyn in the bed he'd shared with his wife. He'd probably considered it the height of betrayal.

Her throat burned with sudden unshed tears. "That's…"

There were no words to explain the hard twist of her heart. Vanessa had been his wife first, and there was nothing she could do to change that. After all, Antonio hadn't chosen her when he'd had the opportunity. Caitlyn was the backup sister.

And Antonio had done something unbelievably

considerate in removing the remnants of his first marriage. He'd told her last night that he wanted to move on. She couldn't blame him for choices he'd made either before the crash or after.

He deserved a fresh start after the horrors he'd endured. If he wanted new bedroom furniture because the old pieces had belonged to his first wife, she'd help him redecorate once a week until he was happy. And keep her mouth shut about how hard it was on her to constantly recall that she was living her sister's life by default.

A clerk approached them the moment they stepped into the hushed store. Expensive plank flooring and discreet lighting lent to the moneyed atmosphere, and the high-end pieces on display even smelled expensive. It would be a Christmas miracle if Antonio walked out of here with a full bedroom set for less than fifty thousand dollars.

"What are you looking for today?" the sales-clerk asked politely. "A new sofa to accommodate extra party guests, perhaps?"

"We're in need of new bedroom furniture," Antonio said as Caitlyn did a double take.

What was this "we" stuff?

"Absolutely, sir." The clerk eyed them both.

"Can you give me an idea what style you might be looking for? Art deco, maybe? American heritage or contemporary?"

"Caitlyn, did you have a particular style in mind?" Antonio asked, and put a palm to the small of her back as if she had every right to be included in the decision. As if they were a couple shopping for furniture together.

"I, um…don't know what you'd like," she admitted, which seemed ridiculous to say when she'd not only studied him surreptitiously for years, she'd also just had sex with him. Shouldn't she know what he liked?

"I'd like something that puts a smile on your face." The look he gave her curled her toes and rendered her speechless. To the clerk, he nodded and said, "Show her everything and make sure she's given the opportunity to pick colors and such. I assume you do custom orders."

Dollar signs sprang into the clerk's eyes. "Of course. Down to the throw pillows. Please call me Judy. And you are?"

"This is Ms. Hopewell," Antonio said smoothly. "And she's the star of this show. She doesn't walk out of here without an entire bedroom set. When she's finished picking what she wants, you let me know and I'll pay for it."

"Excuse us a moment." Caitlyn pulled Antonio to the side. "What are you doing?" she whispered hotly. "I can't pick out your bedroom furniture. It's too…"

Intimate. Fast. Expensive.

"I want you to," he insisted. "After all, you're going to be using it."

She shut her eyes for a moment as she envisioned exactly what he meant by that. "But it's not going to be *mine*. I have a bedroom."

"Not anymore." Antonio's eyebrows drew together as her eyes widened. "I'm messing this up, aren't I? I should have talked to you about this at home. I want you to move into my bedroom. Permanently."

Warmth spread through her abdomen. The staff would know instantly that they were together, so maybe he *didn't* intend for their relationship to be a secret.

But what *was* their relationship? She knew he was the committed sort—it wasn't a surprise that he wanted something permanent. But it would be nice to have specifics. She'd never done this before. Was this his subtle way of asking her to be his girlfriend? Or was this the precursor to a marriage proposal?

Yes. Yes. Yes. No matter what he was asking, the answer was yes.

This definitely wasn't the time nor the place to hash this out, but she couldn't be upset. He wanted her to be a part of his life. Permanently. There was no possible way to misinterpret *that*. Who cared what label they slapped on it? Her heart flipped over and back again, unable to find the right spot in her chest now that everything she'd ever dreamed for herself had fallen in her lap.

He took her hand and squeezed it. "Help me make it a place we can be together without shadows of the past."

Her unsettled heart climbed into her throat as the sentiment crashed through her happiness. If only new furniture could actually achieve that.

She could never be rid of Vanessa's shadow. She was living her sister's life, the one Vanessa couldn't live because she'd died. A life Caitlyn never should have had, despite desperately wanting it. The enormous burden of guilt settled over her anew.

And the worst part was, she couldn't even tell Antonio how she felt, because he definitely didn't need an extra layer of guilt. He couldn't even *remember* Vanessa and it weighed on him.

This was going to go down far worse than the toy store. Picking out a forty-dollar toy for their children didn't carry a million heavy implications the way picking out furniture did.

"Please." Antonio's plea slid through her. "I need to feel as if I'm not still adrift and alone. I need you."

She shut her eyes and let Antonio bleed through her. This wasn't just about furniture. *Nothing* in their interaction was surface level. Or simple. Regardless, there was no point in acting as if there was a choice here. She lacked the strength—or the desire—to deny him anything.

"Okay." She blew out a breath and turned back to the expectant clerk. "I'm ready."

Panic ruffled her nerves. This was so far out of her realm of experience. She was shopping for furniture with a man. With Antonio.

But he was holding her hand and smiling at her

as though she'd just given him the world's best Christmas present. She couldn't let her guilt or the circumstances ruin this. She couldn't let him down.

"Right this way." Judy escorted her to the left, already chattering about fabric and colors and who knew what.

At the end of the day, she'd be sleeping in Antonio's bed. Honestly, who cared what the furniture looked like when her full attention would be firmly fixed on the amazing, sensitive man lying on the next pillow?

As dawn broke through the glass wall overlooking the pounding Malibu surf, Caitlyn curled around Antonio's slumbering form and watched him breathe. The way she'd done yesterday morning. Because it could never be enough. He didn't get any less beautiful, and it was her God-given right to gawk at the man she was sleeping with, wasn't it?

His sooty lashes rested above his cheekbones and his lips pursed as if he was dreaming about kissing her. Funny, that was exactly what she'd dreamed about, too.

So she indulged them both and kissed him awake. "Merry Christmas."

His dark eyes blinked open and he smiled sleepily. "Is it already the twenty-fifth? I lost track."

"We've been busy."

Once she'd gotten over herself, the redecoration effort had consumed them both as they'd laughed and argued good-naturedly over the style and placement of the purchases. Then Antonio had gotten started on artwork, perusing gallery upon gallery until he'd found precisely what he wanted.

Late last night, they'd tossed the final teal pillow onto the couch in the sitting area and declared it done. The finished product looked nothing like the former space. Vanessa's taste had run to heavy and ornate baroque. Caitlyn had selected more simple lines and colors: a four-poster bed with simple square posts. A compact dresser in espresso-colored wood with silver pulls. Teal and dark brown accents.

It had been a magical, breathless few days. But as she'd suspected, Antonio was the best thing in the room. Every day was Christmas, as far as she was concerned.

Antonio rolled onto his side and pulled her into his arms. "Then, Merry Christmas to you, too."

She snuggled into his warm body. "We don't have to get up right away, do we?"

"Not for years and years. The kids won't know about Santa until they're, like, three or four, right?"

She loved it when he talked like that, as if they were a family who would be together forever, come what may. He hadn't mentioned the word *marriage*. But she hoped that was where they were headed.

"Ha. We'll be lucky if they aren't up at 5:00 a.m. next year, pounding down the stairs on their little toddler feet to see what Santa brought."

With a gleam in his eye that was impossible to misread, he winked. "Then, we better make good use of our one bye year."

So slowly she thought she might weep, he took her lips in a long kiss that set off a freight train of heat through her blood.

It was so much more powerful to know what this kind of kiss led to as she fell into the sensual pleasure of his lips thoroughly claiming hers. His tongue was hot and rough and she reveled in the shock of it invading her mouth. Thrilled in it. Because while it mated with hers, it was so unbelievably arousing to recall that he'd also tasted her intimately with that same tongue.

His thigh slid between her legs, insistent and tight against her core. She moaned and arched into the pleasure as sparks exploded under his ministrations. Silently, she urged him on, riding his muscular thigh with small rolls of her hips. She needed...more. But she didn't have to tell him because he seemed to know instinctively what she wanted, as if he could read her mind.

He replaced his thigh with one strong hand and instantly, he found her sensitive bud, rolling it between his fingers as if he'd been born to touch her exactly in this way.

She gasped and her eyelids fluttered shut as waves of heat broke over her skin like the surf on the shore below their window. The man must have a deal with the devil. How else could he be so beautifully built, so incredibly successful at both of his chosen professions *and* be so *good* at making her feel like this?

Murmuring flowery Italian phrases like a prayer against her lips, he touched her intimately and pleasured her until she feared her skin would incinerate and leave her in ashes. Then he trailed his lips down her throat and set that magic mouth on one of her incredibly sensitive breasts. As soon as he curled his hard tongue around a nipple, she detonated like the Fourth of July.

The climax overwhelmed her, tensing her muscles and sending shooting stars across her vision.

"Antonio," she whispered. Or screamed. Hard to tell when her entire body sang his name so loudly, it deafened her.

"Yes, my darling. I'm here." He rolled her to her back and covered her with his unbelievable body, resting his weight on his forearms so he wouldn't crush her.

But it was far too late to prevent that. As he positioned himself to slide into her, joy burst open inside her chest and streamed through her entire body. Oh, she'd been crushed, all right.

Crushed by the overwhelming sensations of being completely, fully in love. That desperation of wanting him from afar—that wasn't love. That was infatuation, and there was no comparison.

Antonio filled her to the hilt, and she rocked her hips to draw him deeper still, a technique she'd discovered by accident last night. And judging by his answering groan, he approved of it just as much this morning as he had last night.

She shut her eyes and savored the fullness of him as he shifted to hit her sweet spot. A sigh escaped her lips. Perfection. Was it always like this, like being touched physically and spiritually at the same time? Or did she and Antonio have a bond other people never experienced?

It was an academic question because she'd never know. This was the only man she'd ever love. The only man she'd ever be intimate with. She trusted him fully, knew he'd be there for her, steadfast and strong. Waiting for him had been worth it. She couldn't imagine being with anyone else like this, opening her body and her heart to another person in this beautiful expression of their love.

His thrusts grew more insistent, more urgent, and she bowed to meet him, taking pleasure, giving it until they came together one final time in a shuddery dual climax that left her boneless and replete.

They lay in each other's arms, silent but in perfect harmony until her muscles regained enough strength for her to move. But she didn't go very far. She pillowed her head on his shoulder and thanked whatever fates had seen fit to grant her this second chance to be with Antonio.

As he'd done yesterday morning, Antonio flipped on the wall-mounted flat-screen TV to watch the news. Habitual, he'd told her when she asked, since returning from Indonesia—to break the silence.

"You don't need that noise anymore," she said and grabbed the remote with every intention of powering it off again.

But in the split second before she hit the button, the news anchor mentioned Antonio's name.

"What are they saying?" He sat up against the headboard and focused his attention on the newscast.

"…the identity of the anonymous donor who had the entire inventory of a toy store delivered to Toys for Tots." The blonde on the screen smiled as a photo of Antonio appeared next to her head. "It will be a merry Christmas indeed for thousands of local children who have this secret Santa to thank. Antonio Cavallari made headlines recently by returning to LA after being presumed dead in a plane crash over a year ago—"

"They shouldn't have tracked down who donated those toys." Antonio frowned. "It was anonymous for a reason."

The newshounds had finally scented Antonio's story due to his generous gesture, which, as he pointed out, should have remained anonymous. He could have paraded around naked in front of Falco and generated less interest apparently, but the one thing he hadn't wanted advertised was what had garnered coverage. The nerve.

A photo of Vanessa flashed on the screen and she flipped the channel. The guilt was bad enough. She didn't need her sister staring at her from beyond the grave. "Enough of that."

But Antonio wasn't even looking at the TV. His gaze was squarely on Caitlyn. "You're very good for me, you know that?"

He tucked a lock of her hair behind her ear and then lifted the long strands from her neck to press a kiss to her throat. She shuddered as he gathered her closer, fanning the ashes of their lovemaking, which apparently hadn't fully cooled.

"I have something for you," he said, his lips sparking against her skin.

"And it's exactly what I wanted," she murmured, arching into his mouth, silently encouraging him to trail those lips down her throat.

It could never be enough. He could touch her every minute of every day, crawl inside her ten more times before they left this bed, and she'd never reach the saturation point.

He laughed and reached behind him to pull a long, flat box from the bedside dresser drawer.

Entranced by the possibilities, Caitlyn ripped off the green foil wrapping paper and lifted the lid. A silver chain lay on the velvet interior.

Antonio withdrew it from the box and held it up so she could see the silver-filigreed initial charms hanging from it. "There's an *A*, an *L* and another *A*."

"Oh," she breathed as her heart surged. "One for each of the babies."

He fingered an *A* and tilted it so the light glinted off the polished white stone set in the center. "When I was in Indonesia, I trained in a makeshift dirt ring. Oftentimes, when we sparred, we'd uncover rocks buried in the soil. I carried one in my pocket when I left in search of where I belonged. It was symbolic of what I hoped I'd find when I got to America. Myself, buried beneath the layers of damaged memories."

Speechless, she stared at him as her pulse pounded.

"I had the jeweler cut and polish my stone. Each letter holds a fragment of it." His gaze far away and troubled, he set the *A* swinging with a small tip of his finger. "If Vanessa had been carrying the babies, they would have died along with her."

True. And horrifying. She'd never thought about her decision to be their surrogate in quite that way. When Vanessa had asked her, Caitlyn had agreed because she loved her sister, but honestly, the thought of getting to carry Antonio's baby had tipped the scales. It had been a win-win in her book, but the reality had so much more positives wound up in that she couldn't feel guilty about it any longer.

He bunched the chain in his fist and drew the covers back from her naked form. She was too emotional to do anything but watch. He knelt to lay his lips on her C-section scars for an eternity, and then his dark gaze swept upward to fixate on her. "My children are a piece of me that I never would have had without you. I cannot ever repay you for what you've given me. This is but a small token."

Tears splashed down her face unchecked as Antonio leaned up to hook the chain around her neck. Everything inside swelled up and over, pouring out of her mouth.

"I love you," she choked out.

She didn't care if he didn't say it back. Didn't care if the timing was wrong. Didn't care if it was only the emotion of the moment that had dragged it out of her. It was the pure honest truth, and she couldn't have held back the tide of her feelings even with a dam the size of Asia.

His gaze flicked to hers and a wealth of emotions swam through his dark eyes. "I wish I could say the same. I'd like to. But it would be unfair."

She nodded and a few more tears splashed down on the teal comforter she'd painstakingly selected. His heart still belonged to Vanessa. It was a poetic kind of justice for her sister. And for Caitlyn, truth be told.

"It's okay. I'm not trying to pressure you. But I thought you should know how I feel."

He gathered her close and held her as if he never planned to let go. "Yet another gift you've given me without expectation of anything in return. You're an amazing woman, Caitlyn."

She laid her cheek over the falcon and listened to his heartbeat. He just needed time to get over Vanessa. She'd *help* him get over her so that strong, beautiful heart could belong to Caitlyn forever. And then she'd be complete.

"Let's go spend Christmas with our family," Caitlyn suggested, and Antonio's rumbled agreement vibrated against her cheek.

The day after Christmas, Antonio couldn't stand his own company any longer and the only solution for his foul mood was to go to Falco. Without Caitlyn.

She sent him off with a kiss and nary a backward glance, as if she really had no clue he was about to lose his mind. Seemed as if he'd done a spectacular job keeping his doubts and trepidation to himself.

He had to do something different to regain his memories. It wasn't fair to Caitlyn that she was stuck in a relationship with a man who had no concrete memories of his marriage and therefore no guideposts to help him move on.

He wanted to. Desperately. He'd hoped finally getting Caitlyn into his arms would do the trick. Instead, all he'd accomplished was to make things worse.

She was in love with him. And the way he felt about her—*wonderful and terrifying emotions* was a stellar way to describe it. When he looked at her, it was as if every star in the sky shined all at once, lighting up the darkness. *She* was his star. The only constellation in his life that would ever make sense. Because he'd done exactly what he'd set out to do. He'd created new memories, new experiences with her.

Surely this was love.

But he'd been in love with Vanessa, or so Caitlyn had told him. Why couldn't he remember her clearly? It seemed wrong to tell Caitlyn about his feelings, his fledging certainty that he was in love with her, too, to promise her any sort of future, when he'd done the same with Vanessa…only to lose all consciousness of that relationship.

What if he did that to Caitlyn one day? What if he got in the ring with Cutter again and the next blow to his head erased his memories of her?

He couldn't stand the thought.

At Falco, he sat in the chair behind his desk. It was a sleek behemoth with a front piece that went all the way to the ground, hiding his lower half from view to visitors. Why had such obscurity appealed to him? He had no idea, but Caitlyn had told him he'd selected it along with all of the other furniture in the office.

Perhaps he'd shopped for furniture with Vanessa, too, as he'd done with Caitlyn. He yearned for his relationship with Caitlyn to feel special and unique. But how would he know either way?

This frustration was useless, and nothing he'd done thus far today came close to handling his memory problems differently. So he picked up the phone and scheduled the CT scan for the following week after the holidays.

It might not help, but he couldn't live in this fog of uncertainty any longer. He'd promised Caitlyn they would talk about the future after the first of the year and he'd been entertaining the notion of taking her to someplace she'd enjoy for New Year's Eve, like Paris or Madrid. Just the two of them.

Antonio pulled the ring box from his pocket and flipped the lid. The fifteen-karat diamond dazzled like a perfect, round star against the midnight velvet. The moment he'd seen it in the case as he'd waited for the jeweler to retrieve Caitlyn's custom-made necklace, he'd known. That was the ring he wanted on Caitlyn's finger forever, as a physical symbol that she belonged to him and he needed her. He imagined her eyes filling with all that sweet, endless emotion as she realized he was asking her to marry him.

But he couldn't ask her until he exorcised the ghost of his first wife.

He pushed away from the desk and strode outside to get some fresh air. Street sounds and the ever-present sting of smog and pollution invaded what little serenity he might have found outdoors.

A flash of red hair in his peripheral vision put a hitch in his gut. An otherworldly sense of dread overwhelmed him.

Slowly, he turned to see a woman approaching him, a quizzical, hopeful slant to her expression. Long legged, slim build, beautiful porcelain face, fall of bright red hair to her waist.

Vanessa.

Oh, God. *It was his wife.* In the flesh. A million

irreconcilable images flew through his head as he stared at her. Pain knifed through his temples.

"Antonio," she whispered, her voice scratchy and trembling. She searched his gaze hungrily. "I saw the news report and couldn't believe it. I had to find you, to see you for myself."

"Vanessa," he croaked, and his throat seized up.

She recoiled as if he'd backhanded her across the face. "What is that, a joke?"

"You're supposed to be dead. Caitlyn told me they found your body."

Caitlyn. Horrified, he stared at the redhead filling his vision. Caitlyn was the mother of his children, his lover. She lived in his house, in his heart…and there was no room for Vanessa. How could this be *possible*?

"I'm not Vanessa, Antonio. What's going on? It's me." Confusion threw her expression into shadow when he shook his head. "Shayla."

The name exploded in his head. Across his soul. *Shayla*.

Laughing, moaning, murmuring his name— dozens of memories of her scrolled through his mind. Her body twining with his. Her full breasts on unashamed display, head thrown back as she rode him, taking her pleasure as if she had done it often, as if she had a right to use his body.

And of course she *had* done it often.

Shayla. His mistress. Vanessa—his wife.

The images in his head of the redheaded woman were so jumbled and nonsensical because he'd had incomplete, fragmented memories of *two different women.*

Eleven

A swirl of nausea squeezed Antonio's stomach as his eyes shut against the shocking revelation. He couldn't look at her, couldn't take the idea that he'd been intimate with her.

He'd been carrying on an affair with this woman. Cheating on his wife with her.

It was repulsive. Wrong. Not something he'd ever have imagined himself doing.

But clearly, that hadn't always been his opinion of adultery.

Gagging against the bile rising in his throat, he turned away from Shayla's prying, too-familiar gaze.

"What's the matter?" she asked. "Aren't you

happy to see me? Vanessa is gone and we can finally be together."

"I don't..." *Remember you.* But it was a lie. He remembered her all too well.

Oblivious of his consternation, she put a manicured hand on his arm. He fought the urge to shake it off because it wasn't her fault he'd forsaken his marriage vows.

His skin crawled under her fingers.

He yanked his arm away and her hand fell to her side as hurt clouded her expression.

"I'm sorry," he said roughly, as pain ice-picked through his skull. "Things are not like you assume."

She cocked her head. "I don't understand what's wrong. You're alive and it's a miracle. Why didn't you call me? I've thought you were dead for over a year. Do you have any idea what I've gone through?"

His short bark of laughter startled them both. "Shayla, I—" God, he couldn't even say her name without wanting to cut out his tongue. Swallowing, he tried again. "I have amnesia."

It was the first time he'd uttered that word out loud. And oddly, naming it, *owning* it, diminished its power. Not completely, but his spine straightened and he nodded at her stunned flinch.

"Yes, you heard correctly," he told her a bit more firmly. "The plane crash dumped me on the shore of an island in Indonesia with few memories. I only found my way home a few weeks ago."

"You don't remember me." Her expression caved in and tears shimmered in her eyes. "Of all the things...I thought we'd pick up where we left—I mean, Vanessa is dead. When I heard you'd survived the crash, I figured you—"

"I remember you," he broke in. "But I didn't until I saw you."

As he'd remembered his lawyer and Thomas. But he hadn't remembered Caitlyn. Or Rodrigo. Which led to the most important question—

Would he remember Vanessa if he saw *her*?

A perverse need to know overtook him.

"I'm sorry," he told the tearful redhead before him, determined to get home and discover what else he could extract from the sieve in his brain. "There's nothing here for you any longer. I'm not in love with you and I never will be."

She laughed bitterly. "Funny, that's almost exactly what you said before you left to go to Thailand. Except you were talking about Vanessa at the time. Didn't stop you from running off on your lovers' retreat."

The words blasted through his head, but in his voice as he said them to Shayla one night.

I'm not in love with her and I never will be. There's nothing left for me in that cold, empty house. The Malibu house. He'd meant the one he'd shared with Vanessa. The one he now shared with Caitlyn and his children.

He'd told Shayla he wasn't in love with Vanessa. Truth? It might explain why he couldn't recall what that had felt like. Or had it been something he'd told his mistress to string her along?

After all, he'd gone to Thailand with Vanessa. Had fathered children with her. All while conducting a hot-and-heavy affair with this woman.

What kind of man did such things? When he'd come to LA to find out who he was, he'd never imagined he'd discover such dishonesty and self-ishness in his past. Who had he *been* before the crash?

Some aspects, like being a fighter, he didn't have to question. That was a part of him. Was being an adulterer part of him, too? A part he couldn't remove any easier than he could stop fighting? He owed it to himself, his children and Caitlyn to learn everything he could about what kind of person Antonio Cavallari had been. So he could chart a course for the kind of man he wanted to be in the future.

"I'm sorry," he repeated. "I have to go. Please don't contact me again. Our relationship, whatever it was, is over."

"Yeah." She sighed. "It has been for more than a year. I mistakenly assumed we had a second chance this time. A real one. You were never going to divorce Vanessa, not with the baby on the way."

That resonated. Divorce wasn't something the man he *knew* he was deep inside would tolerate. "No, I wouldn't have. And turns out there were three babies. Triplets."

Her smile was small but genuine. "Congratulations. Didn't see that coming. Vanessa was smarter than I would have given her credit for. That's triple the amount of child support if you ever did divorce her. I wish I knew how she'd pulled that off."

Child support. A fight with Vanessa where

that term had been launched at him like a grenade... The details slammed through his head. Shayla's name had come up. Vanessa was furious because he'd sworn he'd end things with "that woman," but he apparently hadn't. Then Vanessa had taunted him with the pregnancy, saying it was insurance. Against what?

He couldn't remember that much of the conversation.

"The triplets were an accident," he assured her. "A happy one."

She nodded and he watched her walk away, then strode to the town car so the driver could take him home, where he would get some answers to the mysteries locked in his mind, once and for all.

Once he got into the house, he disappeared into the media room to queue up episodes of the TV show Vanessa had starred in. He should have done this weeks ago. Why hadn't he?

He'd told himself it wouldn't do any good. That his memories of Vanessa were so scattered and fragmented that seeing her wouldn't help. It was a lie, one he'd convinced himself of for his own self-preservation.

Vanessa walked onto the sixty-inch screen

as his pulse thundered in his throat. Slim, red-headed, with delicate features. The way she held herself, something about her demeanor, was horribly familiar...because she looked like a red-headed version of Caitlyn.

Pain knifed through his temples, throbbing in tandem with his pulse.

His memories of Shayla and Vanessa split instantly. Distinct and whole, the snippets of scenes and his interactions with each woman flooded his consciousness. He let them flow despite the enormous shock to his system, absorbing, reliving. And he didn't like the realizations that followed.

Maybe he hadn't wanted to remember either his wife or his mistress. Maybe he'd known subconsciously that he didn't deserve someone as innocent as Caitlyn and he'd suppressed his memories on purpose to avoid facing the dark choices he'd made before the crash.

Grief clawed at his throat.

He had to tell Caitlyn. She should know what kind of man he'd been. What kind of man he still was. Amnesia hadn't made him into someone different. Just someone who didn't remember his sins.

He powered off the TV and sat on the plush couch in full darkness for an eternity, hating himself. Hating his choices, hating that he couldn't remember why he'd made them. Because that was part of the key in moving toward the future—understanding the past.

The door to the media room opened and Caitlyn's dark head poked through. "Hey, I didn't know you were back, but I saw the car and—"

"Come in," he commanded unevenly. "Please."

She was here. Might as well lay it all on the line. The hordes of paparazzi hanging out at Falco had likely snapped a picture of his conversation with Shayla, and he'd rather Caitlyn hear about it from him.

She came into the room, reaching for the lamp switch. He caught her arm before she could turn it on. Dark was appropriate.

"What's wrong?" she asked, concern coating her voice.

It was a painful, unintentional echo of Shayla's question. Apparently, they could both read him well. Better than he could read himself. "I need to talk to you."

How did you approach such a subject? He

hadn't dishonored *her*. But she'd likely be out-raged on her sister's behalf. Regardless, she had to know the truth.

"Sure." She perched on the couch, her features barely discernible in the faint light from the still-open door. He could sense her, smell her light coconut shampoo, and his heart ached to bury himself in her, no talking, no specters of the past between them.

But he'd probably never touch her again. She deserved better than he was capable of giving her.

"I…ran into someone today. A woman. From before the crash. I…remembered her."

"That's great!" Caitlyn's sweet voice knifed through him.

"No, it's not. I was having an affair with her," he said bluntly. Harshly. But there were no punches to be pulled here, no matter how difficult it was to keep swinging.

"An affair?"

Her confusion mirrored his but must have been ten times worse because she'd only just learned of it. He'd had hours to reconcile how truly sin-ful he was.

"Yes. A long-standing one, apparently." Remorse nearly overwhelmed him.

She grew quiet and he wished he hadn't insisted on no lights. Was she upset? She should be. But the darkness left him only his own guilt for company.

"I don't understand," she finally said. "You and Vanessa were happy. You were in love."

"I wasn't. Happy," he clarified. "Or in love."

That was perhaps the most painful realization of all. His confusion about love stemmed wholly from not ever having been in love before. When his memories of Vanessa resurfaced, he'd recognized the truth Shayla had revealed. He hadn't loved Vanessa.

He couldn't compare how he felt now to the past because there was nothing to compare it to. His feelings for Caitlyn were unprecedented.

And he was most definitely in love with her.

Otherwise it wouldn't be breaking his heart to tell her who he was, deep down inside where he couldn't change it.

"Why didn't you get a divorce, then?" Her voice had grown faint, as if she'd drawn in on herself.

"I don't know," he admitted quietly. "Too

248 TRIPLETS UNDER THE TREE

Catholic, maybe. And there was a baby on the way. I'm still missing huge pieces of my memories of the past, pieces I might never recover."

They lapsed into silence and he ached to bridge it, but this was an unprecedented situation, too. She should be allowed to react however she wanted.

"Did Vanessa know?" Her voice cracked and he realized she was crying as she sniffled quietly.

His gut twisted, and her pain was far worse than the pain he'd caused himself. She was hurting. More than he would have anticipated. Of course he hadn't thought this would go over well, but he'd expected her to be angry, not injured. His nails dug into his palms as he struggled to keep from touching her, comforting her. He was the source of her hurt, not the solution.

"She knew." And he wished he understood the dynamics of his marriage, why Vanessa would have stayed in a marriage where her husband didn't love her and was having an affair with another woman. He didn't even remember if she'd professed to love him. "I'm sorry to drop this on you with no warning. It's not how I envisioned this going between us."

They should have been talking about the trip he'd hoped to surprise her with, the imminent marriage proposal.

"It's a lot to take in, Antonio." Her voice fractured again on the last syllable of his name. "I don't know what to say."

Frustration and grief and anguish rose up inside, riling his temper as he tried to reconcile how to get through this, how to move forward when all he wanted was to hear her say it was okay, that she still loved him. That it didn't matter who he'd been. "Say how you feel. Are you mad at me? Hurt? You want to punch me?"

"I feel as if I don't know you. Commitment isn't important to you like it is to me. I wish I'd never slept with you," she admitted on a whisper that turned his whole body cold. "I can't deal with all of this. Not right now."

She slid to her feet and left the media room with a rush of quiet sobbing.

His guiding star had left him in the dark, and he felt further away from finding himself than ever. Ironic that he'd spent so long fighting to remember and now all he wished for was the ability to forget.

* * *

Dry-eyed, Caitlyn fed the babies. It was the only accomplishment she could list for the afternoon.

She rocked Annabelle, staring blindly at the wall as she tried to quiet the storm of misery zinging through her heart. If only she could crawl into bed and shut out the world, she might figure out how to get through this.

But she couldn't. Children still needed to be fed no matter what pain had just ripped a hole in your chest. Christmas decorations still had to be put away, leaving an empty hole where the holiday cheer had been. Life went on, oblivious of how one simple phrase had destroyed her world.

I was having an affair with her.

For years, Caitlyn had envied her sister's marriage. For years, Caitlyn had lived with her unrequited feelings for Antonio. *For years,* she'd suffered crippling guilt over both.

And it was all a lie.

Her sister's marriage had been a sham. The strong, beautiful commitment she'd imagined was an illusion. The man she'd thought so steadfast and constant? An adulterer. Antonio wasn't perfect in the way she'd thought he was, and her guilt had been all for nothing.

Nothing. That guilt certainly hadn't served to keep her out of Antonio's bed. Oh, no, she'd hopped right into his arms with practically no resistance. She'd given her virginity to a man who thought so little of marriage vows that he couldn't honor them. Who thought so little of love that he hadn't considered it a necessity when choosing a wife.

It was reprehensible.

And none of it made *sense.* The awful words pouring out of Antonio's mouth: the admission that he hadn't been in love with Vanessa, the affair, the reasons for not divorcing—they didn't mesh with the man she'd fallen in love with.

She'd known Antonio for seven years. Was she really such a bad judge of character that she could love a man who'd treated her sister like that? How could she forgive any of this?

She wished she could cry. But everything was too numb.

After the babies had been fed, she slumped in the rocking chair as Leon, Annabelle and Antonio Junior crawled around on a blanket in the center of the nursery. It had been only a couple of hours since Antonio had told her. But it felt like a year.

"May I come in?"

Her gaze cut to the door. As if her thoughts had conjured him, Antonio stood just inside it, his expression blank.

For an instant, her heart lurched as she drank him in. Apparently, nothing could kill the reaction she still had to him. A sobering realization. As was the fact that he hadn't tracked her down with some magical solution to the giant cloud over them now, as much as she might wish that such a thing existed. No, he was here because they always played with the babies before dinner. It had become a ritual all five of them enjoyed, and he would still want to spend time with his children no matter what else happened.

Life went on. And they were co-parents of small children. Forever.

"Of course you can come in," she said. "This is your house."

He winced and she almost apologized for the bitter tone. But she didn't have the energy and she wasn't all that sorry. The old Caitlyn would have apologized. The old Caitlyn always had a kind word for everyone and lived in a rosy world of rainbows and unicorns, obviously.

All that had gotten her was devastated and brokenhearted. Why hadn't someone warned her that a commitment had absolutely nothing hidden inside it to guard against being hurt? Actually, it was worse because then you had to figure out how to live with your hurt.

Antonio crouched on the blanket and handed Leon a rattle, murmuring encouraging words as his son crawled toward it. Annabelle hummed as she explored the perimeter of the blanket and Antonio Junior lay on his back in the center of the room, examining the ceiling with his unique brand of concentration.

Not so unique, actually. His father had that same ability to hone in on something and it was nearly hypnotic.

She tamped down the tide of sheer grief. Antonio wasn't who she thought he was. He hadn't been probably since the beginning. She had to get past it, forgive him and get over her disappointment so they could move on. Didn't she?

The clock on the wall ticked loudly, marking off second after interminable second. They bled into a minute, then another. The silence stretched, heavy and thick. But this was how it had to go. They'd play with the babies and eat dinner. Then what? They shared a bedroom. Would they get ready for bed and lay next to each other with the silence and the big letter *A* for *affair* creating an invisible boundary between them?

"I can't do this." She was on her feet, hands clenched in tight fists, before she fully registered moving. "It's like waiting for the executioner's ax to fall."

Antonio glanced up at her, his mouth set in a hard line. It ruined the beauty of his face. He was obviously as miserable as she was. She hated that she noticed and hated even more that she apparently still cared.

"What is? Hanging out with our kids?"

"No. This." She swirled a taut hand in the air to encompass the room at large, but she meant the two of them and the big question marks surrounding their relationship, how they moved forward, all of it. "I can't do this with you. I'm not Vanessa. I won't put up with affairs and I'm not okay with it."

She'd yearned for her sister's life and now she

had it. The whole kit and caboodle. Clearly she needed to be more careful what she wished for. Yet it was such a suitable penance. She bit back hysterical laughter.

"I'm not asking you to be okay with it," he countered quietly with a glance at Annabelle who had pulled up on her crib with a loud squeal of achievement. "*I'm* not okay with it. And you should know, it wasn't affairs. Just one. I told her not to contact me anymore. I don't want anything to do with her."

Did he honestly expect any of that to make a *difference*?

"I need to move back into my own bedroom." Her throat hitched as she said the words and she wished she could take them back, but it was the smartest move for her sanity. "I can't be with you anymore, not like we were."

And there it was. She'd held this man in her arms, cradled him with her body, loved him, slept with him, tasted him. Never in a million years would she have imagined she'd be the one to call off their relationship. In the end, she'd been painfully spot on—she wasn't the right kind of woman for Antonio Cavallari.

Grimly, he crossed his arms. "What will we be like, then?"

She shook her head blindly. "Parents. Roommates. I don't know. I just know I can't sleep in that bedroom. I can't—"

A sob broke through, ending whatever she'd been about to say. Head bowed, she buried her head in her hands, squeezing her eyes shut. She sensed Antonio's presence as he approached, but he didn't touch her.

She wished he would. Wished they were still in a place where he could comfort her. But was glad he didn't. It would only confuse things.

"Caitlyn."

She blinked up at him through watery eyes.

His dark gaze zeroed in on her, overwhelming her with unvoiced conflict and soul-deep wounds. Even now, with these irreparable ruptures between them, she could read him.

"Will you fight me for custody of the children?" he asked softly.

She gasped. "What? Why in the world would I do that?"

"What kind of father could I possibly be?" Resolute and stoic, he stared her down. "I have an uncontrollable urge to decimate other men in the ring. I have amnesia. I defiled my marriage with a tasteless affair. Any judge would grant your petition to take my children and likely award you as much money as you ask for to raise them. If I were you, I would have already taken steps to remove them from my influence."

"Antonio." Her chest constricted as she searched his ravaged expression. "None of that makes you a bad father. Your children need you."

I need you.

But she bit it back. She needed the man she'd *thought* he was, the one who made her feel treasured because he'd chosen her. Because of all the people in his life he could have reached out to, he'd taken her hand and asked her to stand with him when he had gone to Falco the first time. He'd asked her to see the doctor with him. He'd been alone and frightened and he hadn't wanted anyone else but her.

Then he'd destroyed her trust by morphing into someone else. Someone who didn't respect and honor marriage the way she did. Who hadn't loved his wife.

If he couldn't love Vanessa, what hope did Caitlyn have that he could ever feel that way about her? And she wouldn't settle for anything less than a man's love. Yet, how could she trust him if he *did* say that he loved her?

It was a vicious cycle, one she couldn't find a way to break, no matter how many times she went over it in her head. All this time, she'd thought he couldn't tell her he loved her because his heart still belonged to Vanessa. The reality was…indescribable.

Antonio glanced at the babies, and all the love she knew he felt for them radiated from every pore of his being. He was capable of love. Just not loving her.

"No, I need *them*," he said. "As long as you're not going to take them from me, I can handle anything else."

It was a strange reversal of some of their earlier conversations, when she'd been terrified he'd find a way to dismiss her from her children's lives. She knew what that clawing, desperate panic felt like and it softened her. More than she'd have liked.

A harder, more cynical person might have taken the information he'd laid out and run with it, ensuring that she got exactly what he said—custody and Antonio's money. It would be a fit punishment for his crimes.

But she wasn't that person, and as she stood close enough to touch him, close enough to smell his heady masculine scent, her heart twisted.

She still loved him. Nothing he'd said to her today could erase that.

"I will never take your children from you," she promised and her voice cracked. "But I can't have a romantic relationship with you. We have to figure out a way to live together as parents and nothing else. Can we?"

He stepped back, hands at his sides and his beautiful face a mask. "I'll respect whatever decision you make."

Her heart wept over his matter-of-fact tone, as if he had no interest in fighting for her. But what would she have said if he told her no, that it was totally unacceptable to end their relationship? That he loved her and wanted her in his bed, come hell or high water?

She'd have refused.

So here they were. Parents. And nothing else.

That made her want to weep more than anything else that had happened today.

Twelve

Antonio stood outside Caitlyn's old bedroom at 1:00 a.m., hands on the wood, listening to her breathe. God, this separation was an eternal hell.

After two days of staying out of her way, he was done with it.

She was awake and lying there in despair. He could sense it. Her essence had floated down the hall to him on a whisper of misery, and he'd caught it easily because he'd been lying awake in his own bed in similar turmoil.

His headaches had grown worse since they'd been apart, and his pillow still smelled like Caitlyn even after ten washings. She haunted him, asleep or awake. Didn't matter. She was so close, yet so far, and his body never quite got used to the fact that she wasn't easily accessible any longer. He still rolled over in the night, seeking her heat and the bone-deep contentment that came with touching her.

Only to come up empty-handed and empty hearted. The only thing in life that made sense was gone, and it hurt worse than any physical pain he'd ever endured.

The pounding in his temples wouldn't ease no matter how many rounds he went in the ring at Falco. He'd even resorted to a pain pill earlier that evening, to no avail.

The only thing that ever worked to take away his headache was Caitlyn.

He pushed the door open and stepped inside her room. She didn't move, but the quick intake of her breath told him she knew he was there.

"I can't sleep," he said inanely.

Her scent filled his head, pulsing through it with sweet memories, and it was worse than being in his lonely bed without her. This was too close. And not close enough.

It was maddening.

"I'm sorry." Her voice whispered across his

skin, raising the hair. "But you can't come in here in the middle of the night."

"This is my house," he growled as his temper got the best of him. It was the wrong tactic; he knew that. But she was killing him. "I need to talk to you."

"Can't it wait?"

It was a reasonable request for one o'clock in the morning. "No, it can't. Please, Caitlyn. What can I say, what can I do? I'm sorry. I hate that I did something so inexcusable. Can't you get past it?"

"I don't think so." The quiet words cut through him. "We don't have the same views on commitment, and that's not something that I can get past. You told me you believed in forever and I believed you. Now I can't trust you, and without that, what kind of relationship would we have? I'm not like Vanessa."

Why couldn't she see that he didn't want her to be like Vanessa? At one point in time, he'd liked a certain kind of woman, clearly. But he didn't remember why and didn't want to.

He wanted Caitlyn.

And she didn't want him. Because of something he'd done a long time ago. Something he couldn't undo. Something that haunted him, something he hated about himself. He'd surgically extract whatever she objected to if he could. If it would make a difference.

But it wouldn't, and this was one fight he lacked the skill to win.

Without another word, he left her there in the dark because he couldn't stand the space between them any longer. Couldn't stand that he didn't know what to do.

He had to change her mind. She was everything to him and he needed her. Loved her.

For the first time in his life, he was pinned against the fence, strength draining away, and his opponent was too big to overcome.

But he refused to go down for the count. He needed to do something big and drastic to win her back. But what?

After a long night of tossing and turning, Caitlyn gave up at 5:00 a.m. She'd slept in this bed pre-Antonio for over a year and had never thought twice about it. A few days in paradise, also known as the bedroom down the hall, and suddenly there was no sleep to be had in this old room.

And she wasn't fooled into thinking it was the mattress. Her inability to sleep had everything to do with the black swirl of her thoughts and the cutting pain in her chest after shutting down Antonio's middle-of-the-night plea. Closing her eyes only made it worse.

Caitlyn padded to the sunroom and tried to get in the mood for Pilates before Leon woke up. But all she could think about was the first time Antonio had kissed her. He'd backed her up against a wall, literally and figuratively, in this very room, demanding she tell him about love. So she'd spilled her heart and turned the question back to him, expecting a profound tribute straight from the poetry books. An ode to his late wife about his devotion and the wonders of their marriage.

What do you know about love? she'd asked.

Nothing, he'd returned.

She'd assumed he didn't remember love and stupidly thought he was asking her to help him. But really, he'd meant he'd never loved Vanessa. How awful it must have been for her sister, to be stuck in a loveless marriage with a man who wouldn't divorce her solely because of the baby on the way. Instead, he'd forced her to put up with his infidelity.

How had Vanessa done it? How had she woken up each morning, her mind ripe with the knowledge that her husband had been intimate with another woman? Unrequited love was something Caitlyn had a special empathy for. Had her sister cried herself to sleep at night, the way Caitlyn had over the past few days? Why hadn't Vanessa told her what was going on?

Inexplicably, she wished her sister was here so she could bury her head in Vanessa's shoulder and weep out all her troubles. Which was the worst kind of juxtaposition. If Vanessa was alive, Caitlyn's troubles would be nonexistent. She'd still be laboring under the false premise that marriage, commitment, love and sex were all tied up with a big, magnificent bow.

Leon woke up early. While Caitlyn fed him, her mind wandered back to Vanessa and it suddenly hit her that her sister's possessions sat tucked away in the attic. Her sister might be gone, but Caitlyn could still surround herself with Vanessa. Maybe it would help ease Caitlyn's bruised and battered soul.

She turned the babies over to Brigitte, who bundled them up for a ride in the triple-seated stroller, and then escaped to the attic. *Attic* might be a little grandiose of a term—it was really a small, unfinished room above the second floor, accessible by a narrow staircase next to the linen closet.

Caitlyn hadn't been in here for over a year, not since she'd moved the bulk of Vanessa's things after the plane crash. A coating of dust covered the items farthest from the entrance. The boxes near the front had been placed there recently and weren't as grimy. Shortly after Antonio had returned, Caitlyn had asked the housekeeper to pack up the rest of her sister's things.

Sitting down cross-legged, she opened the nearest untaped box. Clothes. She pulled out one of her sister's silk blouses and held it to her cheek. The heavy, exotic perfume Vanessa had favored wafted from the fabric. All at once, Caitlyn recalled the last time she'd smelled it, when she'd been four months pregnant and had come to say goodbye before Vanessa and Antonio left for Thailand.

Tears slid down her face and she suspected the majority of them were because she missed Antonio. Not Vanessa. Apparently, her shame knew no bounds, but he'd been so lost last night. She'd wanted to tell him she wished there was a way to get past it, too. But she couldn't see it.

The clothes weren't helping. Pushing that box to the side, she dived into the next one, which was full of Vanessa's toiletries, including two small, jeweled bottles of her perfume. Caitlyn pulled them out to give to Annabelle. The perfume would likely not last that long, but the bottles were encrusted with real semiprecious stones and the pair would be a lovely keepsake for their daughter.

Perhaps the children she shared with Vanessa were actually the answer Caitlyn had been seeking about how she was supposed to find the strength to live in the same house with Antonio. Had Vanessa considered the babies a good enough reason to stay with her husband despite the emotional pain he'd caused her? Leon, Annabelle and Antonio Junior were certainly the reason why Caitlyn was still here after all. She couldn't imagine not waking up each day and seeing the faces of her kids. It was worth the sword through her heart every time she saw their father to get daily access to her children.

Maybe it had also been worth it to Vanessa to keep her family intact. Maybe that was why she hadn't pressed for a divorce and stayed with Antonio even after she found out about his affair.

Drained, Caitlyn rested her head on the box. Her weight threw it off balance and it tumbled to spill its contents into her lap.

A leather-bound book landed on top. It looked like an old-fashioned journal. Curious, Caitlyn leafed through it and recognized her sister's handwriting.

"Sept 4: Ronald doesn't think the Paramount people will consider me for the lead in *Bright Things*. The role is too opposite from Janelle. I should fire him, but he's my third agent in two years. Ugh. I really want that movie!"

Interesting. Caitlyn wouldn't have considered Vanessa the type to record her innermost thoughts, especially not in written form when her sister had been so attached to her smartphone, but here it was, in blue pen. With all of the email hacking and cloud-storage security breaches that plagued celebrities, Vanessa might have felt paper had a measure of privacy she couldn't get any other way. Feeling a little voyeuristic, Caitlyn read a few more entries at the beginning and then skipped ahead.

Wow, she hadn't realized how much Vanessa had wanted to move on from Janelle, the character she'd played on the prime-time drama *Beacon Street*. Her sister had never said anything about how trapped she'd felt.

It kind of stung to find out Vanessa hadn't confided in Caitlyn about her career woes. Or much of anything, apparently. The journal was full of surprises. Caitlyn would have said they were pretty close before the crash, but obviously Vanessa had kept a lot of things hidden.

Antonio's name caught her eye and she paused mid–page flip.

"I told Antonio about Mark. He totally freaked out, worse than I expected. Simple solution to the problem, I told him. If he'd just stop this ridiculous nonsense about reviving his glory days in the ring, I'd agree to stop seeing Mark. Which won't be hard. He's nowhere near as good as Antonio in bed, but I had to do something to get my stupid husband's attention!"

Caitlyn went cold, then hot.

Her sister had been having an affair, too?

Dread twisted her stomach inside out as she flipped to the beginning of the entry. It was dated over two years ago. Well before Vanessa had approached Caitlyn about being a surrogate. Her sister's marriage problems had extended that far back?

She kept reading entry after entry with slick apprehension souring her mouth.

"Antonio is still really upset about Mark. He demanded I quit *Beacon Street*. I laughed. As if I'd ruin my career for him just so my darling husband didn't have to watch me on-screen with the man I'm sleeping with? Whatever."

And then a few pages later: "Antonio is so horrible. Not only is he still talking about fighting again—which I will not put up with!—he's found what he thinks is the best way to get back at me for Mark. He's having an affair with a woman who looks like me. On purpose. It's so juvenile. He's so not the type to be this vindictive. But I left him no choice, he said in that imperious voice that never fails to piss me off."

Antonio had started his affair in retaliation for

Vanessa's. It didn't change how she felt about infidelity, but it changed how she felt about her sister. And her sister's views on marriage, which clearly didn't mirror Caitlyn's.

Information overload. Wave after wave of it crashed over her. So Antonio had wanted to get back in the ring even before the crash—did he remember that?

Her throat and eyes both burning uncontrollably, Caitlyn forced herself to read to the end. Without checking her strength, she threw the leather-bound confessional at the wall, unable to hold the evidence of how little she'd actually known her sister.

She'd walked into this attic hoping to find some comfort for the task ahead of her—living with a man she loved but couldn't fathom how to trust—and instead found out her sister hadn't been sitting around pining for her husband. In fact, Vanessa had had skeletons of her own in her closet.

Hot, angry tears coursed down Caitlyn's face, and she couldn't stop the flood of grief. Didn't want to. Nothing was as she'd thought. Vanessa had pushed Antonio into the arms of another woman first by forbidding him from doing something he loved and then punishing him via a romance with her costar. It didn't make Antonio's choices right, but against everything Caitlyn would have expected, she had sympathy for him nonetheless.

It was too much. She sank into a heap and wept.

She registered Antonio's presence only a moment before he gathered her into his arms, rocking her against his strong chest. Ashamed that her soul had latched on to his touch like a greedy miser being showered with gold, she clung to him as he murmured her name. She cried on his expensive shirt and he didn't even seem to notice the huge wet spot under her cheek.

His fingers tangled in her hair as he cupped her head gently, massaging with his strong fingers. Tiny needles of awareness spiked through her skin, energizing her with the power of his sweet touch, but she ignored it. He didn't speak and somehow that made it okay to just be, no words, no excuses, no reasons to shove him away yet again.

When the storm passed, she peeked up at his blank expression. "Where did you come from? I didn't think you were home."

"I just got back," he said gruffly. "I…heard you and I couldn't stay away. I know you can take care of yourself, but I needed to check on you. Don't say I should have left you alone and let you cry because that was not going to happen."

"It's okay. I'm glad you found me."

"I doubt that's true when I'm the reason you're crying."

His arms dropped away and she missed them, almost calling out for him to encompass her again with that blanket of serenity. But she didn't. There was still so much unsaid between them. So much swirling through her heart that she could hardly think.

She shook her head. "Not this time. Vanessa—" her deep breath fractured on another half sob "—was sleeping with her costar. Mark—"

"Van Allsberg." Antonio's expression wavered between outrage and bleak resignation. "I remember now. I didn't until you said his name. I almost got in the car to drive to his house and take him apart for touching my wife. How did you find out?" he asked quietly as he sat back on his heels.

"She wrote in a journal." Bitterness laced her tone involuntarily. Vanessa had been very free

with information when the page was her only au-
dience. "I read it. It was illuminating."

Caitlyn's chest hurt as she watched the pain
filter through his entire body anew, as if he was
experiencing it for the first time. And perhaps
amnesia was like that, continually forcing Antonio to relive events he should have been able
to put behind him. Distance didn't exist for him
the way it did for other people, who could grow
numb to the pain—or deal with it—over time.

Unwittingly, she'd forced him to do the same by
jumping on the self-righteous bandwagon, lam-
basting him for an affair that had happened a long
time ago when in reality, she'd known nothing of
the difficulties in his marriage. She'd been judge,
jury and executioner without all of the facts.

She stared at the exposed beams of the ceiling
until she thought she could talk without crying.
"Her affair was your punishment for daring to
express your interest in fighting again."

"I… It was?" Frustration knitted his features
into an unrecognizable state. "I thought…"

His anguish ripped through her, and before she
could list the hundreds of reasons why it was a
bad idea, she grabbed his hand, holding it tightly

in hers as if she could communicate all her angst through that small bit of contact.

"You made mistakes, Antonio. But there were extenuating circumstances."

It didn't negate the sacredness of marriage vows, but it did throw a lot of light on how Antonio's choices had come about.

"That's no excuse," he bit out savagely. "There *is* no excuse. That's why I can't forgive myself."

That speared through her gut and left a gaping wound in its wake.

His distress wasn't faked. Cautiously, she searched his face, his body language, and the truth was there in every fiber of his being. He clearly didn't think the affair was okay now, despite having thought differently back then.

Not only had the affair happened a long time ago, she'd refused to take into account that Antonio wasn't the same person he'd been while married to her sister. As many times as she'd noted he was different, in this, she'd convicted him of being the same.

Amnesia had taken pieces of his memory, and perhaps what was left had reshaped him. Could she find a way to trust the Antonio who had returned to her from the grave and allow the old one to stay buried?

"Antonio." He didn't look at her, but she went on anyway. "You should know something. She said you talked her into going to Thailand as a way to reconnect. You wanted to try again, just the two of you."

He nodded. "I don't remember. But I'm glad that Vanessa died knowing that I was committed to her."

That gelled with the Antonio she'd always known. A man who valued commitment, who despite the rockiness of his marriage had wanted to try again. "I'm sorry I dredged up all of this pain again."

He huffed out an unamused half laugh, scrubbing his face with his free hand. "You don't have to apologize. I remember so little about Vanessa in the first place. Hell, practically everything I know is from things you've told me. So the fairy tale you painted wasn't true. That's actually easier to deal with than the reverse."

"The reverse?"

With a small smile, he stared at the dusty attic floor between them. "That Vanessa was the love of my life but I would never remember what that felt like. That I'd never be able to move on until I properly mourned our relationship. Now I know all I had with her was a dysfunctional marriage that I can put behind me. The future seems a lot brighter knowing that the best relationship of my life is yet to come."

The cloud of pain seemed to lift from his features as he spoke, and she couldn't look away from his expression. It was fresh, beautiful, hopeful.

His strength was amazing and it bolstered hers. "I like the sound of that."

He tipped up her chin and feathered a thumb across her cheek. Lovingly. She fell into his gaze, mesmerized, forgetting for a moment that things were still unsettled between them. Then it all crashed down again: the disappointment, the heartache. The sense that they'd both cleansed a lot from the past but the future still had so many question marks.

Did she have what it took to put the affair behind her, as he seemed to want her to? As he seemed to do so easily himself?

"Caitlyn," he murmured and hesitated for an

eternity, his gaze playing over her face as if he couldn't make up his mind what to say. Finally, he sighed. "I'm miserable without you. Can't sleep, can't eat. I deserve this purgatory you've cast me into, but you have to know that our relationship isn't going down without a fight."

"I'm miserable, too." She bowed her head. "But part of that misery is because I don't know how I'm supposed to feel about all of this. The revelations in Vanessa's journal don't change anything. Marriage is a sacred thing. Sex is, too. I have a hard time trusting that you truly believe that. I have a hard time trusting that if you and I fall into a rough spot in the future, you won't console yourself with another woman."

It was the old adage: once a cheater, always a cheater. Except she'd never thought she'd be wondering how true it was. People could and did change all the time, especially when presented with the best kind of motivation. Just look at her—she'd never envisioned being a mother, and it had taken a huge mind-set change to prepare for it.

He winced and nodded. "I deserve that, too. So that's why I went to Falco this morning and spent hours locked in a room with Thomas Warren and the other executives to hash out the details required to sell Falco Fight Club."

"You...what?" She couldn't catch her breath.

"I want it gone." Grimly, he sliced the air with a flat palm. "It's a brutal, bloody sport. I've got kids now, and limiting their exposure to MMA is always in the back of my mind. But that's not the reason I want to sell."

Sell. The word reverberated in her heart and nearly made her sick.

"Antonio! You can't sell Falco." It would be akin to her announcing she wanted to sell one of the babies. It was lunacy. "That place is a part of you. I watched you fight. You love it. It's as if you were born to be in the ring."

"Exactly. I sign everyone's paychecks. Who's going to tell me no if I say I want to get back into rotation? As long as I own Falco, I have a guaranteed path into the ring."

"You're not making any sense. All of that sounds like a *good* thing. If you want to get in the ring again, I won't stop you. I'll support it," she countered fiercely. "I'm not Vanessa."

Caitlyn would never be so daft as to forbid Antonio to return to the ring if that was what he wanted. Love didn't bind a man's wings and then selfishly expect him to fall in line.

"No, you're not." He knelt on one knee and cupped her face in his hands, holding her steady as he treated her to a beautiful, tender smile. "That's why I'm selling. I want to show you that I can stop fighting. Don't you see? If I can shut off such a deep-seated piece of my soul, I can also remove the part that believed infidelity was okay."

Her eyelids flew shut as she processed that. "Why would you do that just for me?"

"It wasn't just for you. I need to prove it to myself, too." His smile faltered. "As hard as it's been to live without you, it's been even harder to live with myself, knowing that I have the capacity to do something so wrong. This is the only way I can come to you again and ask you to reconsider being with me. How else could you believe me when I say I'd never have an affair again? I needed to prove in a concrete way that I love you."

Stricken, she stared at him as tears spilled over and splashed down her face.

He'd done this for her, as a gesture to show that

he loved her. That she could give him another chance and she could trust him because he'd truly changed.

And he *had* changed. She'd recognized that from the very beginning.

He wasn't the same Antonio. It was blatantly, wonderfully obvious that he'd become someone else. Someone better, stronger, who knew the meaning of love to a far greater degree than she did.

He'd fought the demon of amnesia to find his family and fought to regain a foothold in his life. Antonio had been nothing but brutally honest with Caitlyn from day one, and just as he'd been honest about his affair, she could trust that he was telling the truth that he'd never do that to her. Perhaps she should look within for the root of her issues.

She'd feared for a long time that she wasn't woman enough, strong enough or just plain *enough* for a powerful, complex man like Antonio. Because she wasn't Vanessa and couldn't be like her sister.

But the dynamic between Caitlyn and Antonio would never follow the same path as his first marriage because her relationship with Antonio had no parallel to the one he'd had with her sister. He loved *Caitlyn*, enough to do something crazy like sell his company, which he'd never have considered for Vanessa.

No, she wasn't Vanessa, who had no clue how to love a man like Antonio. Caitlyn did.

Antonio was a fighter. And so was she.

"No," she said firmly. "I refuse to stand by and let you do this. It's not necessary."

"Then, what can I do, Caitlyn?" Frustrated, he started to drop his hands, but she snatched them back and threw her arms around him.

"You can love me." His embrace tightened and she melted into it as all her reservations vanished. "Forever. That's what I want."

She loved Antonio, and forgiveness was a part of that. She wouldn't withhold it a moment longer.

He murmured her name, his lips in her hair as he shifted her more deeply in his lap. "You've already got that. You should ask for the moon because I would give it to you."

"You're more than enough. You're all I've ever wanted."

Antonio stood with her in his arms and navigated the narrow stairway from the attic with all the grace and finesse she'd come to expect from such a magnificent man.

Caitlyn silently said goodbye to her sister and left the past in the dusty attic where it belonged. She had the family of her dreams and she'd never let it go again.

Epilogue

The announcer took the mic and announced, "And by unanimous decision, the winner is Antonio Cavallari!"

With his name buzzing in his ears, Antonio raised his aching hands to the roaring crowd in a classic fighter's victory pose, but his gaze only sought one face—Caitlyn's. The lights of the packed arena blinded him, as did the trickle of blood from his eyebrow, but he ignored it all until he located her in her usual ringside spot.

His wife of six months shot him that sexy, sleepy smile that had replaced her maidenly blush. Sometimes he missed that blush, but not very often, because she backed up the smile with abandon behind closed doors. He grinned back. He couldn't wait to get her alone later. But it would have to wait because a hundred people wanted a piece of the new welterweight champion.

After an hour of interviews, in which he was asked over and over again the secret to revitalizing his career, and then showering through the pain of his cuts and bruises and Thomas Warren's incessant chatter about another champion coming out of Falco, Antonio finally threaded through the animated crowd to press up against Caitlyn's back.

Exactly where he wanted to be.

She leaned into him, and he slipped his arms around her. The silk of her blue dress felt like heaven under his battered hands, but her skin would feel even better, and he let all his desire for her surge through his veins because she could take it. Later, she would beg for him to love her, meet him in his urgency. Because she was his missing piece, and without her, he'd still be wandering through the confusion inside his head, trying to figure out where he belonged.

"Congratulations," she murmured and turned

her head to press a kiss to his throat. "How does it feel to be the king of the comeback?"

"Feels as if it's been too long since you were naked," he grumbled in her ear, careful not to say it too loudly when Brigitte was only a few feet away with the babies.

The au pair had one hand on the three-seated stroller, expertly splitting her attention between her charges and the young featherweight fighter engaging her in conversation. Matteo Long was a rising star in Antonio's empire, and his children's caregiver could do worse.

Caitlyn had continually insisted the kids should be immersed in their father's world so they could learn for themselves the artistry and discipline of Antonio's passion. The fact that she truly understood what made him tick was yet another reason he loved his wife completely.

And his love for her and his children had finally gotten him into a doctor's office to get that CT scan. That had led to more tests and procedures that had eventually uncovered the medical reason for Antonio's headaches—and a solution. He rarely had them these days, which was a blessing for an athlete going after a title.

His private detective hadn't turned up evidence of other survivors from the plane crash. So Antonio had let that quest go—his own amazing story was enough.

Turning in his arms, Caitlyn fingered the chain around her neck where she wore his wedding band while he was in the ring and undid the clasp. Encircling the band, she slid it on his finger and said, "Till death do us part."

It was a ritual they performed often, reminiscent of their wedding ceremony. A tactile reminder of their love, commitment and marriage vows. He'd insisted on it.

Not that he needed any reminders. He still hadn't fully regained his memories from before the crash and had accepted that he likely never would. Odd flashes came to him at strange times, but it didn't matter what his brain resurfaced.

Caitlyn was the only woman he could never forget.

* * * * *